Madeleine Vinton Dahlgren

Chim

His Washington Winter

Madeleine Vinton Dahlgren

Chim
His Washington Winter

ISBN/EAN: 9783337250430

Printed in Europe, USA, Canada, Australia, Japan

Cover: Foto ©Andreas Hilbeck / pixelio.de

More available books at **www.hansebooks.com**

CHIM: HIS WASHINGTON WINTER

Larry Noa...

CHIM

HIS WASHINGTON WINTER

BY

MADELEINE VINTON DAHLGREN

NEW YORK
CHARLES L. WEBSTER & CO.
1892

PRESS OF
JENKINS & McCOWAN
NEW YORK

THIS BOOK IS LOVINGLY
DEDICATED
TO
MRS. ROBERT ANDERSON
IN REMEMBRANCE OF THE
ENDURING FRIENDSHIP THAT HAS EXISTED
BETWEEN
OUR HONORED FATHERS, OUR PATRIOT
HUSBANDS, AND OURSELVES

TABLE OF CONTENTS

CHIM

CHAPTER I

CHIM'S EDUCATION

ALMA AYLWYN taught music in a pretty Pennsylvania town, sometimes called " Little Washington," in contradistinction possibly to the national city of that name.

She was a capital girl, however, even if she did not live in a capital city.

" Little Washington," as it was designated in its early life, is a spot favorable to the outgrowth and the indwelling of much that has made itself known, for it boasts a college of no small renown, and a " Female Seminary," long and well established.

Some men, world-renowned, as, for instance, the magnetic statesman Blaine, "drank deep" at this Pierian spring in youth, at a time when the venerable father of a president's wife was a professor at this " well of learning undefiled."

And this same place has also given to the nation other cabinet ministers and public men; also its philanthropists, like Dr. LeMoyne, and, in fact, an unusual number of clever men and women, who have more or less assisted to regulate the affairs of this spread-eagle nation.

And now we wish to make it known as the picturesque home of a brave, talented, handsome, musical girl, and her adored and adorable dog Chim.

Alma possessed various qualities that fitted her to be the heroine of a realistic novel, although as this story progresses it may be thought that she was not matter-of-fact enough for the absolute requirements of a prosaic age.

But Alma's character rather transcended in its various aspects the present school of fiction, because, in defiance of set rules, she combined the requisites needed to fill pages and pages of the trivial, inconsequential, commonplace events of that every-day life it is so much the fashion to describe with tiresome particularity, combined happily with at least a Promethean spark of fancy, idealism, and soul.

It may seem very strained to say so, but if Alma had not been endowed with this higher nature, which set her apart as something rare, she would not have been the worthy mistress of the wonderful *Chim*.

It was formerly laid down as a rule, that every well-written novel must have its hero and its heroine, so this story, in that respect, opens well—as will presently be seen, amidst the entanglement and disentanglement of the narration, that Chim as the connecting link between the human and the divine element, was, if not Darwinian, at least heroic.

At the tender age of six weeks Chim was presented to Alma by a Virginia gentleman, who, whatever else he may have failed to acquire, did know the points of a good dog.

Chim's education was at once commenced,
and we use the word advisedly and declare
emphatically that this extraordinary being was
not merely trained, but he was educated.

Where the breed has been preserved in
greatest purity, dogs are as a matter of course
carefully trained, and their finest points duly
brought out.

Now Chim, being of an inborn noble strain,
was capable of an astounding measure of development.

He was of the terrier kind, small and elegant
in shape, and his little frame was almost con-
cealed in the masses of long, soft, silky, bluish-
gray hair that covered him from head to foot.

He held his fluffy, feathery tail curved back
with much spirit.

But the grace and beauty of Chim's form
culminated in the exquisite contour of a small,
finely rounded head, with long pendulous ears,
and large expressive eyes, whose mild intelligence seemed to take note of everything.

It was curious, for when one looked at Alma,

one was conscious that she had a history, and her dog, either by reflection or in reality, gave the same impression. It is plain to see that they were two very interesting beings.

Perhaps the name of this dear doggie may be deemed to be an unfortunate one, but Chim had been so named at his birth, by a capricious master, on account of a fancied resemblance to the chimpanzee.

The likeness to this creature, if likeness there was, doubtless existed in the canine's peculiar, almost human look of astuteness.

Could the wee thing have been consulted at the start, a far better name would have been given, but in this our hero shared the common fate of mortals who have to go through life and are ushered into eternity under names not of their own proper choosing. It does seem a little hard, nevertheless, to be born all right, and yet to be named all wrong. Alma at first tried in every way to make Chim answer to a more euphonious name, but without avail. He was docile and loving, obedient and faithful, but for some good reason he had concluded to abide by the name of Chim. Alma thought that he ought to be called "Rainbow," with his silky hair of a bluish-gray sheen and ever-varying tint, but he was too smart to submit to such a fantastic appellation.

"Ah, Chim, thou art wise in thy dog day! —it is strange to see with what strength of mind thou resistest temptation," she said to him.

They sat together in Alma's little room, by the window.

"Dear Rainbow," sighed Alma, letting a pearly tear drop on the top of his curling, shining pate. He was irresponsive.

"Darling Rainbow," she whispered into his fluffy ear, stroking gently the long masses of hair.

He looked grave and meditative, almost half jealous, as if, perchance, some other creature were being addressed. A cat would have purred its own requiem under such magnetic strokes.

"I will try it once again," thought Alma.

"Beloved Rainbow," she urged, resting her damask cheek caressingly on his head.

But the little fellow lay inert, and seemingly unconscious of the endearment.

"It's no use," she said. "He has a right to his own name, as it defines his individuality. Chim, sir," she cried, rising with a somewhat displeased air.

At once he responded and the whole of his little form grew instinct with virile life. He seemed to be one big nerve, and each particular hair was electrified. He bounded, rolled upside down, yelped, shook himself, and almost articulated his delight. Then Alma's quick, musical ear, at once caught in Chim's voice a reflex of human tones.

She gazed wistfully into his soulful orbs of eyes—

"How deep they are," she soliloquized; "not painted eyes, or surface eyes, like those of so many people, whose lives from the cradle to the grave merely skim along on the surface froth and foam of an irresistible tide."

What indeed was the peculiarity of those big eyes that made them a riddle, and yet a blank that defied penetration? They were so mysteriously veiled, like a prophet of Khorassan.

"Is he *né-coiffé?*" thought Alma? "Is he a mascot?"

And Chim mentally answered, "I am your mascot."

Who can lift the tantalizing haze that hangs over those eyes?

"Chim," she says, "I command you, *see as I see!*"

He barks "*yeh—yeh.*"

"It is very human," mused she reflectively—"it means assent. It means 'yes.' *It is* 'yes,' a lisping yes, such as a child might give," she presently exclaimed. "Come my darling, try again," she urged "—slow—plain—'y-e-s.'" Chim certainly had it—stammered perhaps—but said "y-e-h."

So the morning lesson closed with one word of the diapason of sound reclaimed by the canine tongue.

"I have," thought Alma, "spanned by a threadlike bridge reason and instinct, and 'yes' is the connecting link—it is affirmation. And yet the chasm itself is not bridged, for my reasoning faculty is conceptive, while my dog's power must be imitative. Ah, Chim! I fear we are as far apart as ever."

Chim barked "y-e-h."

"My darling," said Alma, bending intently over him, "cannot the ethereal film that covers your eyes be brushed away? Is it the cobweb bars of your prison, dear? Why are you thus encaged? Is there no help, Chim?"

Chim articulated distinctly a yelping "y-e-h."

"Lovely," said Alma, squeezing him tight in her arms. "You are, as the world goes, a dog—nothing more. I am a woman. You are born to perish. I am born to life everlasting—ah, dear, must you be blotted out utterly? Is there no immortal spark of life?"

Chim looked dreamy, shut his eyes, concentered himself, and was silent, being too

wise to grapple with the infinite. It's queer in
how many ways the antithetical occurs; for
instance, *silence* is alike the refuge of the wise
and the idiot.

"Ah, doggie," continued Alma, "I'm afraid
you're automatic, or only at best a galvanized
force of some kind. Chim, did you evolute?"
The dear little thing winked, blinked, shook
out the masses of hair, yawned, stretched out,
got up and turned round three times, then
calmly settled himself for what is called a
"catnap," which dogs are very fond of taking.

"Ah, dear, I understand you," said Alma,
"you mean that my talk is tiresome, you little
rascal. I am but teaching you the origin of
your species—and you end all in sleep; well,
that may be the end of all for you."

After a time they took a walk over the
green hills that environ Little Washington.
Alma was meditative—Chim was frisky.

The next day and the next, and the next
after that, and so for five successive days, there

were music lessons to be given. Oh, the mortal fatigue of it all! Has no one ever thought of the torturous fate of a music teacher? Of a being whose ears are trained and sensitive, and whose greatest happiness is in concord of sweet sounds, yet who is doomed day after day, month after month, year after year—yea, for years covering a lifetime to be jarred by discord, always to hear the quavering notes of beginners. Never to be able to listen to really good music. To know that so soon as the favorite pupil can play well, that your task is over. Then to begin again, only to shudder anew over failures. What invention of purgatorial pain is this?

"Yes," mused Alma, "in my grandfather's old home, I remember to have seen some wonderful bronzes.

" What could have become of them? They represented three musical devils. The big demon sits astride of a huge drum, the face of which represents time as a clock. He tries to quench eternal fires by clamor. He bends fiercely over, beats his **devil's** tattoo until the very nails of his toes lengthen into **talons, and** the skinny, batlike hands take on the **sem-** blance of claws, **yet never for an** instant can he cease.

" A second imp stands bending an aching ear **to a violin,** from which **he** draws double **dis-** cordant tones, and the hard lines of his eager face contract in pinched dismay as the **sensi-** tive sense is forever lacerated.

" Yes, forever, without pause, intermission, or rest, must he be thus tortured. And his **long fingers** convulsively **wind** themselves **in** agonizing tension **over the finely waxed bow.**

" The third **doomed one shows his endless** pain as he bends over the relaxed and broken strings **of a** lyre. Eternally his hands are **bruised by** snapping cords, **and** the echo of the jarring sound pierces his brain. Again and again he clasps with swollen, **forceful** fingers the aimless octaves. Naught **for him but ever-** lasting collapse.

" Quivering with extremest nervous tension,

the attenuated feet are transfixed into the yielding molten earth."

And Alma's musical soul shivered as she recalled these bronzes that had made such a deep impression on her when a child.

"Can this be," thought she, "the special hell of the lover of music, who has put the heavenly art to base uses in life? Can there be a sheol, where there is the ocean's ebb and flow, of surging, lapping, tumultuous waves of inharmonious sound without rhythm—without surcease? Ah, let me not then complain if I suffer from discord now, but, embracing my cross with patience, make of it ascending scales to Heaven."

Then Alma recalled that past when, as a flaxen-haired child, she had always loved music, and later on her talent was developed.

Now her gift was the resource upon which she must depend.

Oh, what memories came with the faint recollection of that dear rambling old house!

It all seemed so unreal, so like the fevered and inconsequent events of a nightmare dream.

First, there was her father's death. Up to that time there had been a broad sunshine in which one might have bathed, it was so tangible—yet she was so young then that she rather remembered the sudden shadow through her mother's pain.

After that loss and the leaving the big house there came the wasting away of the dear mother, and the well-remembered sorrow of her loss.

She was aroused from the stupor of this great darkness by the cousin who now lived in her grandfather's big house sending her to a boarding-school to be educated for a music-teacher.

Just to think of it—not for the joy and the love of her art, but for grinding work!

How it all came about she never could understand. Her cousin was cold and stern, and had written her that "there were business complications." But except through his letters he was a stranger to her.

After all, Alma had the instinctive philosophy that youth and beauty give.

And way down in her heart she knew intuitively — that is, she knew without knowing that she knew—that she must sooner or later, on some fine day, draw one of the big prizes in the lottery of life.

Nor was she far from wrong, because there does always seem to be a wheel turning out prizes for the young and the fair.

" After all," laughed Alma, pinching Chim's ear, " I have you, my pet, and more docile, obedient, sensitive and faithful than any human friend."

And as Chim nodded approval, she added: " But you need education. That I will give you, and you shall go down in history as the most learned of your race. Through you, dearie, the canine nature shall reach a peg higher— through the canines the equines— through the equines the felines will stretch up to a higher plane. Yes, attain it through Chim and myself."

One sees at a glance what a brave girl Alma was—how very intelligent, nay, learned—almost the equal of a Vassar girl, indeed, if she did have to teach music to earn her daily bread.

" In fact," said she, standing, not before her mirror, but beside her window, " I have my ambitions; let fate do her worst, I shall not succumb. So, courage—I place my hope in Chim."

Succeeding this revery, and the resolve that grew out of it, Chim was taught daily. He went to school. What may not be accomplished with such a teacher ?

It is said that cultivation expands the human brain.

Even educated pigs become interesting. In fact, we know quite a number that are more or less so.

It is a solemn fact, although not a scientific one, perhaps, that so great was the magnetic *rapport* established between Alma and Chim that the positive pole of her brain found its negative pole in his noddle, and there was thus existing a free current of communication by which a seeming intelligence was transmitted.

It is said that the particular method of transmission discovered by Alma was, the rubbing the dog between the eyes with the forefinger, which digital pressure always had an hypnotic effect. But after a time, so busy was Alma in her otherwise unoccupied hours, so absorbed and interested in experimenting with Chim, that she absolutely forgot to remember how lonely she ought to feel.

And right here, one may as well confide it, Alma had a little secret, which was valuable; it was this: that outside of religion there is no surer road to positive content than to ignore one's self. She had observed that more than half the desolation, the excessive grieving, the morbid sufferings of men and women come from this never-ending thinking about one's self.

It is the hibernation of the ego that sucks

out all the fresh juices of life and leaves **even**
the young stranded on the shores of time, **as**
crouches the lean and gaunt bear, recumbent
in his darksome lair.

Chim looked **forward to** his lessons **with**
eager pleasure.

There was so much to attract in the paper
bag of crackers, the saucer of milk and **the**
lumps of sugar that at the **end** of the lesson re-
warded this apt scholar.

The dog's improved articulation, under the
daily tuition of this dear, accomplished vocal-
ist was surprising. **He** could readily **bark**
"yes" **and** "no." His bow **was** Chesterfieldian
—just the accepted form for good breeding—a
slight, slow inclination. **His** snarl, like that
of the man of fashion, conveyed the most pointed rebuke, while his welcome to those who
were worthy **of it,** was diffuse and **generous.**
Should he by any mischance have **met a poor**
relation, he knew how to pass him by **with a**
sniff. Was he properly introduced **he could**
scent the air with cordial approval. Did he

happen to be among strangers, he knew how
to become totally indifferent to their presence.
This educated whelp had every fine point of
fashionable society at his toes' ends—even to
the sheathing of his claws, until he could
scratch with effect. It is not to be denied that
the puppy is admirably qualified to take a high
place in the *beau monde!* His attitudes are
Delsartian and expressive of easy grace, his
moods capricious and senseless, his reasoning
powers in abeyance, his impulses those of his
breed, and his conversation refreshingly unin-
telligible.

Evidently, art had assisted nature to make
Chim a great social success. Was he destined
to waste those remarkable powers in a restricted sphere? We shall see. It is the part of a
wise dog to prepare for greatness, as it may,
inevitably, sooner or later be thrust upon
him. To be sure, with the human race the
thrusting is apt to come in another world,
which is a great advantage, inasmuch as it
comes upon a higher plane. But our hero,

being only a dog, had to look more to present
results. How was this brought about—how?
Mark my words, that is, if you can understand
them. Alma had intuitions, owing, probably,
to the big old house of her grandfather in Virginia and the early perceptions resulting from
her training when she was a little tot. She
knew that to be well received Chim must be
just the least bit of an Anglomaniac, and so
she taught him to take a thimbleful of high
tea at 5 o'clock. Naturally, being, after all,
only a puppy, he didn't take kindly to slops,
but he was persistently squeezed into this refined taste, by being tied tight in a small arm-
chair, where, posed judiciously and firmly on
his hind legs, he was taught how to hold a cup
and saucer daintily 'twixt the forepaws, and
sip tea scalding hot, without a tear or a gulp.

But the culminating triumph was the dawd-
ling way in which Chim shook hands.

Oh, Jupiter! what a graceful dip and curve
he had! Slowly twisting a forepaw by a
seeming dislocation from the shoulder-blade,

the limb, rigid to the first joint, suddenly became flexible from that intersecting point downwards, then hung for one brief instant limp, before it darted into a jerk. It was something immense!

And still the little wonder literally grew, although neither mistress nor skye-terrier were, I fear, understood by their immediate circle, as they deserved to be, as indeed usually happens with the meritorious. Columbus was not understood in his time, nor is Shakespeare to this day! And perhaps it may have weight to state here, that Chim let Alma know, during the hypnotic process, that he was a Baconian. But let that go: we have now to deal with a certain law of nature, that where there is light, a shadow falls. So, out of the bright dawning light of a new era for all dogs, all beasties, over one miserable dog there fell a deep shadow.

It came about in this wise. Near where Alma boarded was a green meadow, through which ran a silent brooklet, and here the dear

girl loved to take her pet, where, reclining on
the gentle slope of its verdant bank, she
amused herself with the playful but surprising
pranks of the canine.

On this woeful day, Alma was sent for, to
see some one about music lessons, and when
Chim would have followed her, she bade him
remain where he was in the open air, until her
return. At first the dog ventured to go with
her, but Alma would not tolerate disobedience,
and spoke sharply to him, when with an appealing look, and a pitiful whine he fell back
upon the grassy sward, and Alma went on
without him.

Had he no premonition of danger?—no finer
sense of coming evil?

Be that as it may, when Alma, who was de-
tained somewhat longer than she expected,
returned—Chim had disappeared.

The most prolonged and careful search gave
no clue to the missing treasure.

Alas, the last glimpse poor Alma had had
of her darling was the sorrowing gesture, the

faint whine, with which he had collapsed upon
the grass.

Alas, alas! Chim, with the superior prescient
ken of his race, had foreseen the impending
peril and tried in vain to avert it.

Alack-a-day! He had preferred obedience
to ruin and fallen a martyr to duty.

What can be more painful than to have to
chronicle the perfections of an amiable being,
who by an inexorable chain of events is thus
suddenly snatched from view!

Yet not wishing to impair digestion, or har-
row sensitive hearts ruthlessly or needlessly,
I can at least draw a kindly veil over the sharp
sorrows of Alma, and perchance likewise over
the unmerited sufferings of Chim, at this most
dolorous, most unforeseen interruption of their
united loves and lives.

CHAPTER II

THE course, not of true love, but of this true story, now transfers us from the pleasant town of Washington, to the enchanting capital of that name, where various things transpire of moment to narrate.

Here we find Lennox Montague, a youthful practitioner, amid the pleasurable excitement of opening an office for the transaction of business, and the satisfaction he experiences is something akin to that of the *débutante* when she is first ushered into the *beau-monde*.

Both are just emerging from a chrysalis state, and coming into new conditions, involving success or failure.

This captivating young lawyer was fair to look upon, and slight, but in no wise effeminate,

because he was mild of aspect and of graceful
appearance.   In a word, he was slender but
not shallow.

His amiable expression was inherited from a
gracious and charming mother, and his alluring address the result of careful domestic
training.

The finest school of manners comes from
the successive training of three generations,
although more may be permitted, and this
advantage Lennox Montague had had.   This
gave him what might be called a fascinating
intelligence.   He had grace, ease, strength,
with quick intuitions that led to prompt action.
The desire to please inherent in refined na-
tures made him a decided social favorite, and
he blended the rare qualities of being exact in
business and punctilious in society.

It may seem strange to say so, but in reality
both these characteristics have precisely the
same basis: that is, close attention to little
things.   In business this habit is of first importance, and it does not seem to be generally

understood what very momentous matters occupy society.

One readily agrees to entrust one's affairs to a person who, besides being otherwise competent, does not neglect the smallest detail.

These admirable traits and his mental gifts caused this youth to be alike trusted by men, and a favorite with women.

He had been a diligent student at Harvard, and graduated at her law-school, well equipped for the career he had chosen, and old family ties had induced him to come to Washington.

At first he had entered a leading law firm, in order to familiarize himself with local legal forms, and now, having well served this apprenticeship, he was ready to launch out for himself.

Of course his office was on F street, and a very modest room it was, for it takes a moderate income to meet an F street rent, and although Lennox Montague was what is aptly called " well off," yet he was not wealthy.

The old families of Washington were always

taught to pray, "Oh, Lord, give us neither poverty nor riches," and Lennox belonged to that honored and honorable *tiers-état*.

But every one predicted that in the near future he would be rich, he was so clever.

As yet, Washington is not too spoiled to refuse to take an interest in trivial things, and at times the more trivial the deeper the interest, and so it made quite a little stir that one of her social favorites had taken an office for himself, and really meant business.

So rare a thing could scarcely be credited, except upon inspection of the premises, and not a few society women called upon the young attorney as soon as he was established in his cozy office.

Miss Featherweight came to have an important codicil of a forgotten ancestral piece of old blue Canton china, willow pattern, added to her will, and she declared that the aforesaid office was "just too cute for anything," and she was a good judge of cuteness and china. While Mrs. Akmé, who called as an old friend of his mother, in order to encourage him, remarked, that " the place had an air of reserved force, as if work would be done there," and even the inordinately rich Mrs. La Fayette de Noo, happening to hear at some " tea " that Mrs. Akmé had been there, descended from her carriage, and as she stood in the doorway of the minute room, took in, as she thought, the situation at a glance, and in her most condescending, patronizing way, said to Mr. Montague, " Although I find the room miserably small, it is, I am sure, quite big enough for *you*, and, Mr. Montague," she added, as she sailed out in a stately way, " pray say to Mrs. Akmé that I, too, have called, and that, so far as being your friend goes, we are in *a rapport.*"

It was a way Mrs. La Fayette de Noo had, when she wished to be particularly impressive, that she always improvised scraps of bad French.

The truth is that this worthy lady's conversation was a picturesque bit of mosaic work of modern Europe; where, again to use her own words, she " had for several years incontinently rambled." It was so good of her at last to come home, and—again we quote—"furbish up Washington a bit."

General Alibi had jauntily sauntered in, and Dr. Mensana came to inspect the spot, and see if it "harbored microbes," and to suggest "fumigation as a prophylactic."

Then a rich widow had asked him to look after "some troublesome complications that pressed upon her, as she came to Washington to enjoy society, and these affairs were tiresome."

And all this came to pass before he had had time to do more than place two or three chairs, a table, and a hat-rack in the office, for while he was thinking about getting a revolving arm-chair and a suitable desk, he found himself a busy man.

It seems to be an understood thing, that in the beginning one must wait for clients, so it is pleasant to be able to mention that in this case, from the very outset, clients waited for Mr. Lennox Montague.

And this happened in dear, delightful, traditional Washington, that is ready to pin her faith to the representative of her three past generations, in case the man himself is of any substance to pin onto.

It was cheering to see a good name, a good education, a good head, and good morals appreciated.

Almost at once he had to have a typewriter, and it was refreshing to find a homely boy and not a pretty girl employed to fill that function.

Mr. Lennox Montague was really wise beyond his years.

The question of a comfortable arm-chair had been satisfactorily settled, but Mr. Montague still pondered over the more difficult problem of a roomy revolving desk.

Happily, any revolver of a dangerous nature was not to be an article of needed furniture. We have outgrown that and the demijohn of whiskey, in the inventory of Washington offices. Now we have patent refrigerators and Potomac water-filterers in their places.

Finally, all was complete except that ample

old desk with pigeonholes and secret drawers and revolving top that shut down upon its lore when not needed, just as a lawyer should.

Such a desk as was wanted had not yet been found.

" I tell you what, Montague," said Dr. Mensana, whose specialty was giving advice, " you'll never get a grandfather's desk, except at an auction or at Zimmerman's."

" A hint to the wise " is enough, and just such a desk as he had a mental vision of was purchased the very next day at Latimer's, having been shipped for sale by a Baltimore commission merchant who had sent word it was an heirloom of an old Virginia home.

His dream had at last materialized, and the desk was put in position so that the light from the one front window should fall upon it.

The happy owner was arranging his files of papers therein with gleeful contentment, when Mrs. Akmé, who had a most friendly interest in his success, came in to ask him to formulate a charter for a new club for her, and to consider it as "business."

"Give me legal phrasing, Lennox," she said, "for I like precision."

But as she spoke she stopped, and, looking at the desk and then at her young friend, who was beaming with satisfaction, she said:

"I see you have found a desk to suit you."

He flushed a little as he replied:

"It is really curious, my dear Mrs. Akmé, that I should be so elated over the finding an old piece of furniture. I know it's foolish, but this quaint old desk stirs me as strangely as if it contained the family archives."

Mrs. Akmé looked very grave as she said to him: "Do not wonder at it. There must be a correlation of forces somewhere: an occultism about this seemingly inanimate thing which will probably at some future period develop into a potent factor in your life when least looked for."

Lennox Montague, in spite of himself, felt the influence of these words so earnestly spoken. He had a great respect for Mrs. Akmé. He knew her to be a woman of a singularly penetrating intelligence and of high aims. There was nothing narrow-minded about this man, and because he did not happen to understand a thing was with him only a reason for thinking it over.

What could she mean? He felt that the explanation would involve much that did not appear on the surface. He now remembered that when he had last met this lady she had told him that she was "reaching a higher plane, and daily becoming emancipated from prejudice." So he supposed, which was correct, that she was applying new tests to things around her.

Therefore he answered: "It may well be that there is an occult reason why I should be so in love with my desk. Now, if indeed it was a beautiful young lady the occultism would be readily understood."

And he laughed.

Mrs. Akmé smiled and said: "That's just

it, Lennox — allow me to call you by your
mother's name, for I loved her well. Ysolde
Lennox was a woman to love."

"Ah, *do, do* call me Lennox," he said, earnestly, his emotional face full of feeling.

"Well, my dear Lennox, as I said, how do
you know but that this desk that moves you
now so strangely may in some way be connected with a charming girl who will one day make
you happy?"

"The suggestion is delightfully romantic,"
said he. "I shall hug my fancy the closer
and sigh for future developments."

"Do not be impatient," she said, calmly.
"Through repose of soul we unravel myste-
ries. Happiness is relative; it is alone found
by the wise."

Again Lennox looked puzzled. Mrs. Akmé
caught his expression, and knew that he was
mystified.

"I perceive," she said, "that you do not
understand me. Come to the society that
meets once a month at my house, and the

wisdom-religion will make itself more manifest."

"Thanks, dear Mrs. Akmé, for the privilege.
May I ask if your society has a name?"

"As to that we are as yet undecided," she
replied. "It is truth we seek, and all ways
are alike to us that lead to this end. We
ventilate our theories without restriction, and
out of this mind attrition we expect to evolve
light."

"Why," said Lennox, startled by what was
to him a new idea, "the casting off of mind
trammels is the dawning of a new era."

"You are quite right," she said eagerly.
"Only think of the freedom. Each one may
proclaim his own theory. There is no limit.
For instance, I myself have been led into a
train of speculative thought, connected with
theosophy. In fact I am philosophically led
to believe that the canine race marks the real
progress of civilization."

"The canine race!" exclaimed Lennox, in
undisguised amazement.

" It may seem absurd," replied Mrs. Akmé calmly, "and this is not the place or time to defend a thesis. Nevertheless my theory may be logically defended. You see at once, Lennox, one of the uses of our society. We sift all things. It is the alembic through which we filter truth. But your morning hours must be given to business, not philosophy. So for the nonce good-bye."

Really Lennox Montague had a half headache as he saw her graceful retreating form finally disappear from view, as she sank back amid the cushions of her luxurious carriage, and drove off.

He felt as if he were living in a nondescript age, that was, perchance, about to be hurled into chaos, with all the old moorings cast off, and the world afloat without foothold, as was Noah's ark.

Lennox Montague's mother had been a Catholic, and although at her untimely death his tender years had left him uninstructed in her faith, yet he had always rested in the conviction that she was right, without indeed knowing anything about it, more than the general idea, that truth must rest in unity, and could not be hydra-headed, and speak with a confusion of tongues.

In the midst of this painful revery, he mechanically seated himself at the magnetic desk, which had in a certain way given rise to a conversation fraught with somewhat indistinct recollections of his mother.

Never before had such a yearning to receive her blessing filled his soul, and as he buried his face in his hands, she seemed to stand beside him as his guardian angel, and without her loving care the world was very lonely and empty.

But at noonday in a business office on F street, the hour and place are totally unsuited for other than matter-of-fact routine, and so, indeed, he was presently recalled to himself by the somewhat jarring strains of a hurdy-gurdy, turning off a lively tune, which was accompanied by the alternate chirping, whistling, and singing of an odd little old man, who appeared heartily to enjoy his Bohemian mode of life.

His involuntary, meditative mood, being thus rudely broken in upon, he got up and stood at the window, looking out at first in an absent-minded way.

But his attention was speedily arrested by the strange antics of the thick-set, white-haired, white-bearded, and precise figure, who had the solemn air of a Turkish dervish, and yet cut the most absurd prim pirouettes, to mark each musical roulade of his organ.

The stolid face of the slovenly boy who turned the crank, and stood as unmoved and seemingly as uninterested as if he were throwing potatoes in a vegetable bin, or doing any other merely mechanical work, was in sharp contrast with the comical whirling of the dancer.

It is surprising how very quickly a crowd gathers in a city, for almost in the time it takes to tell it, the trio were surrounded, the third performer being a wee dog, who might have been a monkey, so nimble were his movements as he carried around in his teeth a basket, into which jingling pennies were thrown.

As each coin rattled in, the queer creature made an inclination of his woolly head meant as a bow, and hugely appreciated by his audience, who greeted them with shouts of laughter.

The intelligent canine understood and was exhilarated by the wild applause as a human being might have been, and when his master said to him in broken English—"Cheem zay yees, I give Cheem dis"—holding up a dry mouldy-looking biscuit, the wretched puppy, evidently hungry, or kept so to better enact this *tour-de-force*, leaped for it, making leap after leap, barking a chorus of distinctly en-unciated "yes, yes, yes."

A street crowd, after all, is a critical audience, and detects shams more readily than a fashion-able crush, and this was a genuine novelty, and no mistake, and was greeted by clapping of hands, and cries of "Bully for you!"

" It's a comfort," thought Lennox Montague,
"that the masses know a good thing when
they see it, and have none of the hateful *nil
admirare* about them of the world of fashion;"
and so thinking he clapped too, observing
which the curious little old man, very ungrate-
fully breaking through the admiring circle
around him, commenced a special series of
capers under the window for the young lawyer's particular benefit.

Both master and dog knew assuredly that
they were now performing for a trained eye,
and they both did their very best for their
selected critic.

" The old man," thought he, " is equal to a
whole curiosity shop, but the being he calls
' Cheem ' half mesmerizes me ; he is positively
weird." The dog, as if divining his thought,
stopped an instant, and gazed at him in a
yearning, wistful way with his wonderful wide-
open eyes, and it did look as if tears filled
them. So might an enchained captive implore
from his prison-barred window to the passer-by.

" Ah," thought the youth, "the appeal is all the stronger because it is *mute*. Anyhow, I can't stand *that sort* of look," and suddenly he remembered the original remark of Mrs. Akmé about the canine race, that had led to their strange conversation that very morning and induced his recent meditation, which was interrupted by this very dog.

The concatenation of circumstances struck him as uncommon, and he suddenly decided to try and secure this surprising "canine," as a present to his mother's friend.

Acting upon this impulse he beckoned to the pair to come in, which they instantly did.

If one wishes to see an "allegro" in celerity of movement, just try asking a street beggar or a hurdy-gurdy man, or a scissors-grinder to walk in. Their breezy mode of entrance puts to shame the tired, *blasé* gait of the pleasure-seeker. There are so many novel sensations one never gets because one plods on in the old ruts! And so one makes life stupid, because one is selfish.

"Gooda day," said the Italian, as he stood bowing very low.

"All right," said Lennox Montague, drily, as much as to say to the quaint object before him, "Listen to me and keep quiet."

The tone told on master and dog, and they both stood perfectly still.

"Tell me, fellow," said he, "how much do you ask for your dog? of course you will sell him?"

"Per monish, yees," answered the organ-grinder with a scraping bow, "Cheem one vara, buen' cagnolino."

"Well, if I buy this dog you call 'Cheem,' how much? Be quick about it—I'm in a hurry."

The man looking quite unconcerned, said, "Feefty dollare."

"Nonsense," said Lennox; "where did you get him, anyhow?"

The thrust some way went home, for there was a slight wincing, which the quick eye of the young attorney noticed, as he added, "Is he yours to sell?"

"Durty dollare," was the dogged reply.

"Not at all," replied Lennox. "Is he yours, I say?"

"Den ten dollare," was the sulky answer.

"Here it is," said Lennox Montague, handing this true specimen of the conscienceless lazzaroni the money.

"*Bene, bene,*" he said, chuckling, and thrusting the price of "Cheem" deep down in his pocket, walked out, whistling, without a word or even a parting glance at the dog.

"Why has he sold his performing dog so cheap?" thought Lennox; "evidently he wished to escape detection in some way, or I'm no judge of human nature, or lawyer either." And the dog! He certainly bore no love for his master, and if ever actions which "speak louder than words," meant anything, the desperate joy of the poor little skye-terrier said, "I am saved."

During the bargaining for the price set upon his curly head, he had looked from one to the other with wistful earnestness, and when finally the man disappeared, his ecstasy knew no bounds. He crouched at the feet of his new master, and laid his head caressingly against him.

For the first time Lennox then perceived a dainty collar around the creature's neck. It had been covered over by masses of long hair pulled down. And on this collar was engraved " *Chim.*"

" As I supposed," thought Lennox, " the terrier was picked up. He is some fair damsel's pet, who doubtless is inconsolable without him."

" Well, Chim, you shall have a good mistress until the lost one is found."

At 5 o'clock that afternoon Lennox Montague sent up his card to Mrs. Akmé, who was sipping a cup of tea, meditatively, beside a glowing samovar.

He had had Chim carefully dressed for the visit; that is, he had hired a barber to have the dog properly bathed, combed, curled, cleansed, and perfumed.

So Chim was as presentable as any well-bred puppy could be made, and feeling very lively in consequence of the needed ablutions, when he made his bow to Mrs. Akmé. A society training is invaluable, and Chim was at last and again in his proper sphere. He at once put on his company manners, and when Lennox Montague quietly introduced him as " Mr. Chim, just arrived from the celestials," the well-bred darling made a very graceful bow.

"The best bow-wow I have ever seen," said Lennox laughing, but his smile died away to an expression of dazed wonder, when Mr. Chim, scenting the well-loved beverage to which he had been accustomed at that very hour, quietly leaped into an arm-chair beside Mrs. Akmé, and posing upon his hind legs extended his forepaws, and, taking hold of her cup carefully, drained it daintily to the last drop.

Mrs. Akmé turned deathly pale, and Lennox Montague sprang to his feet, fearing she was about to faint—but in a moment recovering herself, she embraced Chim lovingly, exclaiming, " Is this a waking vision ? Have I indeed found the connecting link ? "

CHAPTER III

BUNCOMBE HEREFORD belonged to an old Virginia family, and that was the best there was about him. Detached from his ancestry, he was essentially a man to be avoided, but unfortunately, when in the general plan the current of his life ran counter to the specific object he had in view, and any unlucky wight got caught in the glittering meshes of his frauds, there was not much left of his victim by the time this bloated spider relaxed his hold. Yet his webs were mathematically spun in the sunshine, athwart the highways, and were very fair to see, and being held legally, one could not escape their toils without inanition and complete exhaustion. When he made ready to spring upon an object, fastening

57

down upon him, and closing in the transaction, the wretch was inevitably ruined. But while his small dealings kept him well in practice, and had, by their uniform success, enlarged his perceptions of the possible, yet these attempts were as mere by-play compared with the daring of his big deals. He was a ruthless financial Napoleon, a scourge, as have been some generals called great, who strode onward to their goal over the trampled dying and dead.

Several of his operations bordered on the marvelous, for he had mastered the art of financial levitation, or walking upon air, knowing, as well as Simon Magus did, how to hold himself up on nothing, or perchance he worked his marvels by producing an hypnotic effect on other minds.

It is said that he commenced his astounding career by having an entire paper town laid out, buying the land he speculated with, not, as stupidly honest people might imagine, with money, but giving his notes therefor, these bits of paper secured by a deed of trust on the land, with a small cash payment to confirm contract, borrowed from a friend. Then he had a really excellent picture made, paying the artist with one of his worthless notes, of a flourishing manufacturing town, with volumes of dense smoke issuing from the tall tops of many factory chimneys, and there was a vista of a fine water power, hinting at limitless capabilities in that direction. It is surprising how many people like attractive pictures and Quixotic windmills, and all such investments! Then, with the rapidity of an able commander, turning the enemy's flank when he foresaw that the inevitable collapse must come, he hastened to scoop in the thousands invested upon his representations, let the trust deeds revert the land to their owners, and promptly took advantage of the bankrupt law.

Under this protecting ægis he rested and recruited, meantime manipulating the gullibility of those who seek rapid methods of getting rich, and when the time had come, got himself elected president of a syndicate for the building of an air-line railroad, to be run by a motor upon a new principle.

Having had some experience regarding the stability of real estate, his first aim, before the road was built, was to buy up all the land at a low figure, adjacent to the proposed route ; again his notes were issued in payment, but being backed by a syndicate, this little affair was readily managed.

It is amazing what power this cabalistic word "syndicate" has. One would suppose it was the initiation pass-word of a terrible, oath-bound secret society.

It really is a hideous car of Juggernaut that rolls over the length and breadth of the land, with that vacuum inside that nature abhors, and its relentless, sharp - edged scythes of wheels cut a clean wide swath of desolation.

Mr. Buncombe Hereford had now become this mysterious Adonhiram, with the secret symbols.

His fiat went forth that the thousands upon thousands of acres of worthless land that bor-

dered upon his imaginary air-lines, were inex-
haustible mineral lands, worth at a low figure
a thousand dollars an acre, and the endless
thousands of American dollars were paid for
them.

At this opportune moment, he deserted bodily, bag and baggage, to a real built railroad
company, that, getting frightened at the clam-
or of the air-line, bribed Mr. Buncombe Hereford by the offer of its presidency.

The astute managers of this rival road ignored the risk of installing a traitor over their
company, being more than pleased at the boom
given their stock by the crash of the so-called
syndicate.

The retiring president kicked the bucket of
the syndicate that had brought him up out of
his hole back again to the bottom of the well,
and at last, with real millions in his coffers, became a distinguished citizen—a punctilious,
church-going, phylacteried Pharisee!

Any villain, be he behind prison bars in this
world, or fallen into the bottomless pit of the

next, is disagreeable to contemplate, but not
so exasperating as when he swings aloft, astride
his beam of success, having secured a tight
grip on the good things of this world, as had
Mr. Buncombe Hereford. However, there is
always a limit to the finite, and no one could
insure him against renewed insolvency in the
future. But we have now explained far enough
to be ready to observe that everything in this
narrative must be subordinated to Chim, and
that if we have, with perhaps tiresome minute-
ness, hinted at the colossal manipulations of
Mr. Buncombe Hereford, it is because of their
being of some interest to us, as incidental to
the dog. Otherwise it would be quite unpardonable to introduce such a monstrous sham
into these pages.

Now about the time that Chim arrived in
Washington, trotting along on his little four
legs, or the proverbial "shank's mare," behind
a hurdy-gurdy, our very successful ex-syndi-
cate, now railroad, president, arrived in a luxurious special car. He came in solitary state,

inasmuch as poor **Mrs. Hereford had** been, so it was whispered, confined in a lunatic asylum for several years.

It was openly said that our magnate might, at any time that he so wished it, easily procure a divorce on the ground of wilful desertion. But then, he was so chivalric, and she, only a woman!

For some time previous to his coming, the principal real estate agents of Washington had been looking for a very big house, for this very big man, who had bottled up a very big plan to help the government of the United States of America build an elevated rapid-transit railroad that was to make a direct run to Duluth. Of course it would be nothing to Crœsus, but it might be very much to the North American continent.

It was a merciful thing that the hypnotic spell he exercised did not cause the White House to be offered for his occupancy.

With coy coquetry and sensational acumen, this magnificent showman did not put in an appearance during the initial proceedings of the early winter, but he waited until the so-called " season," congressional and social, was fairly under way. But with the onrush of the New Year, he arrived.

It is perhaps mortifying to have to say so, but Washington is merely beginning to build palatial homes, and the only furnished house that could be procured was, of course, very inadequate in many ways, although in some respects it suited very well, for, as we at first mentioned, this *chevalier d'industrie*, if one may be allowed to hint plainly, was a real born cavalier.

Being thus to the manor born, he knew that the best way to entertain was the exclusive, or dinner-giving method, and that the mahogany round which he would place his guests must be old, the pictures on his walls must be of exceptional merit, and have an actual or an invented history. The china and glass must have been well cared for by successive generations of butlers, and the wines must have the aroma of choice old vintages.

He knew very well that there was a magnetic effect in the *antique*, skillfully manipulated, that could be effectively applied whenever he was ready to pull the wires and set his mannikins to work.

Thus bent on making use of family prestige, he remembered that in a certain spacious home that he had wrested from a widowed cousin, through some *hocus-pocus* of a tax sale, or pretended sale, there was precious store of carved and chippendale furniture, some fine paintings, old bronzes, china and glass decorated and engraved with the family crest, and rare wines. He had written an order to have various of these evidences of former grandeur shipped on to Washington, and placed in the house he had taken there.

Now, unscrupulous men are very apt to have faithless menials to do their bidding, and the fellow in charge of this fine old place, who was underpaid anyhow, had, after a logic his employer would have perfectly understood, indulged now and then in selling to curiosity dealers such pieces of furniture as could be conveniently packed and sent away.

The creature satisfying his conscience by the reflection that he was thus making his own pay about what it ought to be.

He had only recently sent a very curious old desk up to Baltimore that had been used by a former proprietor for his private papers, where its sale brought him quite a handsome sum. But, happily for him, Mr. Buncombe Hereford only gave a general order, and, in fact his recollection of his uncle's old house dated back to his early childhood, when he on several occasions had gone there with his mother, who was an only sister of the proprietor.

He had therefore a very indistinct ·remembrance of any particular pieces, which was a lucky circumstance for his dishonest agent.

As it was, there was quite as much shipped as was needed for the already furnished Washington house, in order to produce the desired effect.

It seems very inappropriate, when writing

about this supposed-to-be-many-times-a-millionaire, to mention these little things, and we have only done so by explaining that these arrangements were simply as means to an end.

Having thus pleasantly domiciled Mr. Buncombe Hereford, whose expected arrival had produced no little commotion in certain quarters, one must for the present leave him and those who were interested in him and his movements.

Miss Featherweight, for instance, was always on the *qui vive* for distinguished arrivals. Also Mrs. La Fayette de Noo, who had not breathed the rarefied air of upper-tendom long enough to escape, on a trying occasion like this, heart flutter and brain muddle.

This lady had for so many years of her early life been subjected to the penetrating odors of boiled cabbage and stewed onions, that she never could exactly tone down to the mild fragrance of the violet, or the delicate *bouquet* of some rare vintage. Her trouble was what the philosophers would denominate "a want of adaptation."

It is a queer thing how each poor mortal makes a voodoo of what he or she don't understand, and we all stand quaking under the shadows of our own fetich.

Let us pray for strength to come boldly out into God's glorious sunlight, so as to see things as they are. Then we could lay aside our inch-worm measure.

.   .   .   .

We left the lovely Alma Aylwyn disconsolate and lachrymose over the mysterious disappearance of her dog. The human heart is so constituted that just in proportion as one is poor and lonely the affections cling all the more closely to whatever of comfort remains.

Thus Alma, who was quite alone in the world, had lost a loving friend in Chim.

There was much sympathy expressed and felt for her loss, and there were various conjectures as to what could have become of the wonderful skye-terrier.

Some boys—for boys see everything—re-membered to have noticed an organ-grinder pass through town, and go away on the na-tional road that day, but no one could aver that he had a dog with him.

Certainly his loss left a sad blank in Alma's life, and some months wore away heavily enough as the summer faded into autumn.

There is a proverb, "It never rains but it pours," although why such an untruth as to the physical world should be proverbial is strange.

But as applied to that grouping of events that forms the thread of human destiny, it is more apt to be true.

So it came to pass with Alma that, in the midst of her mourning for Chim, she was told that after the Christmas holidays—that is, at the close of the term—two of her best scholars would leave town; and while she was much worried at the loss of pupils who greatly inter-ested her, and also at the serious diminution of her means of support, she received a short, curt letter from her only relative.

This relative was the cousin who had, as he told them, paid their debts, and taken her mother's home as payment, and who had, besides this considerate act, borne the expenses of her education at school after her mother's death, until she was sufficiently instructed to teach.

Although, since leaving school she had not received any direct aid from this relative, yet she always had the feeling that if the worst came to the worst she might apply to him; and to know that one has a staff to lean upon is restful, even if one never leans.

But this harsh letter rudely dispelled all illusions in that direction.

It was written by the secretary of this unfeeling man, and simply had his signature attached, which made it all the more cutting.

In it he informed her that, understanding she was now prepared to support herself in consequence of the musical education he had so generously given her, she must no longer expect a continuance of his charity, but must in future become self-reliant and self-supporting.

This was the substance of this unkind missive, which closed with a formal " truly yours." Ah, how cruel, how unfeeling, how heartless !

And it was most galling for a high-spirited girl to be so rudely reminded that she had been an object of charity.

Yet this exasperating letter had this good effect, that it caused Alma to take a very serious and careful review of the situation in which she was placed, and to weigh all the conditions of her position.

The result was so discouraging that she felt she must take counsel of some one more experienced than herself.

In the midst of this painful perplexity she suddenly recollected a benevolent old gentleman who had at one time filled a conspicuous position for his country, but had now retired from active political life.

She recalled how kindly he had once spoken to her, and told her that when he was in Washington city he had, a score of years before, on several occasions met her honored grandfather.

At the time she thought with a heartache
how that word "honored," applied to her
grandfather by one who had himself held po-
sitions of trust creditably, would have pleased
her dearest mother. Oh, how little a word is,
and yet how much !

No sooner had all this come to her mind
than she reproached herself not to have paid
her respects to this excellent man before, and
she at once decided to take counsel of him.

Just here it must be observed how constantly it occurs in life that all the best things we
do, and the things most fruitful of good results, are not of our own planning in any way,
but are sure to come to us when needed. This
takes place because we are in God's hands, and
there is His Providence that arranges for us.

Certainly Alma's visit to this philanthropist
was timely.

She was well received, her little story list-
ened to with attention, and the letter read by
him with indignation.

The name of this unfeeling cousin was not

unknown to him, and he sat for some time, evidently thinking the matter over.

"I cannot understand, Miss Aylwyn," said
he very kindly, "how your mother could have
so entirely lost what must have been a very
handsome estate inherited from her father.
It was always understood that your grandfather was a wealthy man."

"Ah, no!" sighed Alma.

"And you tell me that your mother died
poor, that this cousin has educated you, and
that now, through his heartless desertion, you
are absolutely dependent on your own efforts
for daily bread?—it seems incredible."

Alma's tears, which, at this recapitulation of
her sad fate, she could not restrain, were her
sole answer.

"Oh, I beg of you, dear Miss Aylwyn, don't
cry," said he hurriedly; "I know it will happen
so, that women are left poor, and do really
lose everything. And yet," he added, "this
ought not to happen, nor does it often happen
without their being cheated—"

"Oh, pray, sir," interrupted Alma, "don't say that! There was no one who would have cheated us, I assure you."

"Yet," said the old gentleman with a slight elevation of his shaggy eyebrows, "you have this cousin, who is very rich."

"Oh, yes," replied Alma; "but only see how good he was to us."

"I see," said he, sarcastically; "very kind; shows his big heart in this letter. Eh?"

Alma again cried, for the letter had nearly broken her heart.

"Oh, don't, don't cry!" begged he nervously. "I really can't think, if you will cry. Nothing upsets me like a woman's tears."

"Pardon me," said Alma, half smiling through her tears; "I am so sorry to distress you."

"All right," said he; "now be a brave girl, and, take my word for it, things will come round just as they ought to be, sooner than you think for. I'm no longer young, and I've often seen this sort of thing happen."

" Oh," said Alma, "just the kind words comfort me so ! "

" Never mind," said he. " There now, already I have a bright thought for you. You shall go right on to Washington City."

" To Washington City ! " she exclaimed in a tone of such blank amazement, that the next moment they both laughed.

"Yes, to Washington City," he repeated. " You see, I have been retired from public life these many years, for I'm no longer exactly a young man."

" Men," thought Alma, " must be more nervous about their ages than women; if I were as old as he is, I think I would just say I'm old."

" But," he added, " I certainly have influence enough left to set afloat into smooth seas such a small craft as you are, and one so trim."

" How nice he is ! " thought she.

" My idea is this," he continued; " you must get a clerkship under the Government. You are, in a way, entitled to ask it, for your respected grandfather was well known as a public-spirited, patriotic man. Go, pack your trunk, my dear Miss Aylwyn, and come to me to-morrow, when I will have some letters for you, and give you any needed instructions."

"What a proof," thought Alma, "that it is always the unexpected that occurs," as, expressing her thanks warmly, she hastened back to her room, to follow his advice implicitly.

Yet it loomed before her as a huge and perilous undertaking. "Will it end in shipwreck?" she could not but ask herself. "Oh, mother, mother, come back, and be my guardian angel!" she prayed. And the wide world is full of motherless girls, with desolation and yearnings for a mother's love in their hearts.

Counting over the small sum of money which was her worldly all, her heart sank. Yet she was fortunately too innocent, too ignorant of snares, to measure the perils of her future.

The succeeding day, when she called upon her kind friend at the appointed hour, he had several letters written to influential people who had political influence; but, most thoughtful of all, one addressed to a woman of social position, whom he had known from her childhood —in fact, he had been her father's friend. He explained to this lady exactly who Alma was, and precisely how she was situated, and he begged of her such protecting care as she could so perfectly extend to an unprotected girl, who had to fight life's battle under such pathetic circumstances.

These letters were handed unsealed to Alma, one by one, with very explicit instructions.

"Go," he said; "the moment you arrive, to present your letter to the lady. She will advise you where to get a safe boarding-house, and I am sure she will allow you to refer to her, which will enable you to get a comfortable home. Then present these other letters. These gentlemen will help you, but it may take some little time before they can procure you a clerkship, for a situation under the Government is like a cheque on a banker. In order to draw upon it there must be a *quid pro quo*." And

he laughed just a little, as if mentally reviewing various official *quids* he had known about.

"Well," he continued, "if at the end of, say,
three months, you fail to get an office, come
back here, Miss Aylwyn, and we will manage
another year to have a regular place provided
for you in the 'Female Seminary,' as a teacher.
Meantime, you must live, and you must be
freed from the carking care for daily bread,
which kills the young, I believe, quicker than
the old, so here, my dear young friend, is a
letter of credit for you on Riggs & Co.—"

"A what, sir?" said Alma in undisguised
astonishment.

"Oh, a mere business form!" replied the
beaming philanthropist. "Go to the bankers,
Riggs & Co., with it, and they will let you draw
upon me for fifty dollars a month, for three
months; you see it's a mere nothing—to pay
your board bill."

"Oh, no, no!" said Alma, now shedding a
flood of tears. "Really, I can not—I can work
for this money, my dear, good friend—"

"Tut, tut, child!" stammered he, getting very red in the face; "didn't I tell you it worried me to see you cry? take it, and good-bye."

"But I can't, I can't," said Alma, wringing her hands; "what would mother have said? I love you, good, kind friend, for this thought—I'm grateful—it's not that—"

"The fact is," said the old man in a husky voice, "you *have* to take it. Well, it's a debt I owe your grandfather. Eh? do you see now? Good-bye, and God bless you," and so saying, he opened the door, and fairly hustled her off.

Amid Alma's excitement, she had sense enough to know that the only "debt" that existed was that due to humanity, and she accepted the aid with a heart glowing with gratitude, and the firm resolve at some day to repay it as a loan.

As the noble-hearted man abruptly closed the door to conceal his own embarrassment, she did not hear his soliloquy of, "The Lord forgive me if I told the poor child what Mrs. Opie would have called 'a white lie.' A debt to her grandfather! Ha, ha! I call that a good joke. I well remember the stately old gentleman, whom I met at a dinner at Ogle Tayloe's in Washington. Why, it's enough to make that proud cavalier turn over in his grave, to have me send his daughter's child to Washington, and pay her board-bill. There's been rascality somewhere. Ah, what of that villainous rich cousin?"

CHAPTER IV

ALMA FINDS A HOME THROUGH CHIM

THE year was very old, and Christmas near at hand. Congress was in session, and Washington, the capital of manifold attractions, was now in the heyday of her charms. Her political, her official, her fashionable, her literary, her artistic, her scientific life was in flower, and this brave city, the central point of statesmanship, of intrigue, of the commonplace, of original thought, of abstruse investigation, of art culture, of earnest search after truth, was now in full panoply, having put on the whole armor of a leading factor of civilization.

No wonder that the sayings and doings of this city of bewildering contrasts, representing alike the nation and the age, should be given first place in the news columns of the country.

Yet, apart from these news notices, and sheltered from the casual gaze, as are wheels within wheels, may be found inner circles peculiarly and distinctively typical of the freedom of thought and its expression, that characterize this people, and in these reunions may be found, as in the kernel of the nut, the real pith and substance of the outside movement of the times.

One of these centres existed in Mrs. Akmé's drawing-room, which had long held an acknowledged preëminence as a nucleus, where every thinker was welcome to ventilate his thought.

Mrs. Akmé represented much that was paradoxical, and herein, perhaps, was the power that she undoubtedly wielded over others.

As to lineage, she readily counted several generations of estimable people, each of whom had been looked up to in their day, and this gave her the advantage of being quite sure of herself, so that she was not in the least afraid to recognize or even cultivate the acquaintance of those whom she fancied. As the world goes, this special privilege accorded to birth is inestimable and a talent to be accounted for, received from the Lord. It enables one fearlessly to give social rights to merit, and to go beyond the narrow boundary line, within which so many cringe.

Then Mrs. Akmé had, in addition to a highly respected name, inherited considerable means, which enabled her to be independent. Having money enough for her purposes she could afford to give this adjunct its proper place in the social scale.

Everyone bears a cross in this world, and Mrs. Akmé's was loneliness.

She was a childless widow, and felt her situation all the more keenly as the recollection of the good husband and interesting little daughter she had lost were lasting and at times painfully vivid.

Not having faith in any religion, but being a woman of strong and deep feeling, these sorrows had impressed her manners, which were grave and serious.

But she was of an active temperament, true, in earnest, seeking for light, and from her habit of striking out in all directions for information without an assured guide, she had amassed a surprising conglomeration of half-digested theories.

During several years she had been passing through successive phases — " planes," she called them—and her conclusions of to-day by no means indicated what they might be to-morrow, because her creed was " progress."

At the particular time we are writing about, although she disdained to be pinned down and classified under any name, like a dissected butterfly, yet in the various conclusions she had adopted, others might have called her a bit of an agnostic, slightly a theosophist, wholly a metempsychosist, and having a leaning toward the Christian scientists.

So it may be seen that this excellent lady was holding her mind and soul like a sieve, ready for the reception, the careful straining,

the percolation and the infiltration of the ac-
cumulated theorems of the ages.

Such is the rarefied height of this nineteenth
century, from which the long-despised feminine mind, like the weird *She*, images in seeming youth and freshness the decay and the
effete problems of a buried past.

Mrs. Akmé, it cannot be denied, had her weak
points, and yet such a paradox was she, that in
her very weakness was a sort of strength.

For instance, she was inclined, without knowing it, perhaps, to be very exclusive, yet her
quite special tastes ran counter to everything
conventional.

Access to her drawing-room was difficult,
yet there were points that proved an " open
sesame."

If an invitation was desired on the score of
wealth or fashion, she would decline with the
remark that such a person could give nothing
that she desired to have; but if she was told
that any one was clever and original, she would
not fail to make them welcome.

The motive for her selections may have been all right, but the result was a collection of the most dissimilar and, at times, incongruous elements.

Once a month, on Sunday evening, this society had a meeting in Mrs. Akmé's parlors, the object of which was really, so far as she was concerned, the diffusion of knowledge.

But the real outcome was to bring together minds holding the most advanced opinions.

Curiously enough, these meetings were looked forward to with infinite zest, not only by the members of the association, but also by the society people, whom they affected to ignore.

It is a queer thing that the fashionable world is so perverse as to unmercifully snub those who show an anxiety to cultivate them, but at the same time they knock at the doors of those who affect an utter indifference to their movements.

So, in spite of Mrs. Akmé's expressed wish, that merely fashionable people should not come, they made a point to make her *salon* a society event.

She was aghast to find that it was a craze to be literary.

Yet, as Mrs. Akmé was very kind-hearted, she tried to find consolation by reflecting, that although these unfortunates could in no wise benefit them, yet perhaps they might raise the tone of their social life.

But she overlooked the fact of the brainlessness of fashion, and that one might as well send tracts to Timbuctoo, as to reclaim frivolity by literature.

On this particular Saturday morning Mrs. Akmé was sipping a cup of cocoa at high noon, admiring Chim, who sat beside her, also holding a tiny cup of this nourishing beverage, and chatting with Lennox Montague, who had brought her a business paper to sign.

" To-morrow evening, Lennox, at 9 o'clock," she said, " I shall expect you, for I wish then to thank you, before our society, for the priceless gift of this wonderful creature, whose rare en-

dowments illustrate and confirm my most cher-
ished theories. **Chim, too, wishes to thank you**
for rescuing him from a terrible captivity—"

Chim, upon hearing his name, made a very
sedate **little bow of assent.**

At this moment the **door-bell** rang, and
presently the butler handed her a note and **card**
upon a silver salver.

Mrs. Akmé disliked **to be** disturbed **during**
those hours that she deemed she had a right to
claim as her own. We suppose every one has
the same feeling.

"Harman," she said, **as she took the note,**
"I have several times explained to you, not to
permit my mornings **to be invaded;** " and, addressing Lennox, she **added, "this is one** of
the trials of a Washington life."

Meantime the door by which the lackey
entered was ajar.

What was **it that** seemed **so** strangely **to**
agitate Chim? The dog, a moment before
so placid, now **hastily** put down his **cup,** sniff-
ing.

His mistress instantly noticed his movement, for it was her latest fancy to make this creature her inspiration.

"There is something occult in this uneasiness," she said to Lennox, who began to have a suspicion that she was *non compos*. "Pardon, if I read this note, it may be a missive from one of the Silent Brothers."

Chim had now put his finely pointed nose between his forepaws, and was quivering in every limb.

Mrs. Akmé, agitated by his agitation, read the note hurriedly. It was the kind letter from the dear old gentleman of Washington, introducing Alma, and commending the unprotected girl to her good offices.

"Strange this should be needed," she said to herself, "for I knew her courtly grandfather when I was a young girl, and he was thought to be a man of family and fortune."

Harman still awaited orders. "Show the lady in," said Mrs. Akmé.

Another instant, and Alma entered.

With one piercing cry, that was human in its intensity, **Chim** bounded from his chair, with a sudden spring, and rolled over and over at the feet of his beloved, long-lost mistress, fondly licking her hands in an ecstasy of joy —while she, poor child, in amazed delight, called out, "Chim! Chim!" and, kneeling down, pressed her darling, long-lost pet to her wildly beating heart.

This affecting scene lasted some moments before Alma arose trembling, but still clasping her treasure in her arms.

Mrs. Akmé was exceedingly pale.

Never before had Lennox experienced such mingled emotions of surprise and admiration, for Alma was a beautiful girl, and the scene made a picture for eye and heart to dwell upon.

What peculiar sensations overcame him as he instantly realized the astonishing circumstance, that he, too, was one of the actors in this little drama, he having found and rescued the dog, and thus prepared the way for this rapturous meeting. And now he was the witness to their happiness. He felt for the first time in his life as if he might be the hero of a fairy tale, to whom was confided the clue that threaded a labyrinthian maze.

But Mrs. Akmé was ecstatic, as one who is suddenly transported beyond the boundary line, and ushered into another world.

The visible faded away, and she grasped at the invisible.

To her highly exalted imagination this meeting was not only a revelation from the spirit world, it was a positive command.

Her penetrating intelligence connected the links of the mysterious chain of events, and her generous heart at once conceived a project.

It was evident that the wonderful dog belonged to this fair girl, who now stood before her, a beaming, lovely picture, with the adorable creature nestled close to her heart, as he peered out at her from underneath his overhanging silken curls, with a kindly but yet a defiant air.

Fidelity is the sublime attribute of the dog;

the virtue his race typifies, and she knew that his first lealty belonged to his mistress.

Yet this being meant more to her soul-life than any joy or sorrow that could come to her, for he was the exemplification of that which she had eagerly sought.

He was the embodiment of a principle.

She felt sure that she alone had divined his secret; she alone knew him to be a wonderful incarnation, and she alone must guard this astounding evidence of metempsychosis. At all hazards—all sacrifices—she must keep him near her; he must be watched over for the sake of truth, and out of her reverential belief in the wisdom-religion.

There was so much awaiting proof that could only be solved through this marvel of trans-migration.

A thousand, thousand, incoherent thoughts were hers, which formed themselves, more rapidly than can be conceived in the telling, into one firm resolve.

That was, that she would never, never part

with this being; and in order to retain Chim, she would adopt Alma, to whom he belonged, as her own daughter.

The young lady was interesting and very lovable, and it would be nice anyhow.

Fairly trembling for fear of a refusal, Mrs. Akmé approached the homeless orphan, and embracing her, said in the most captivating way:

"Dear child, I welcome you as my own daughter—stay with me, and be mine."

As she uttered these persuasive words, the poor lady was overwhelmed with an overpowering recollection of her own fair child, always mourned for, although lost years ago. This lamented child would, if living, have now reached Alma's age.

Subdued by these conflicting emotions, the proud, the collected, the self-reliant, thought-leader rested her head, as if for solace, upon the shoulder of this beautiful girl, with a protecting arm thrown lovingly around her waist.

"Madam, dear, dear madam—" was all that

Alma could say, as she felt as if her heart would burst; and Lennox Montague, understanding with the quick intuition of a refined nature that the improvised scene was too sacred, the reality too extraordinary for any witness, quietly withdrew.

The last glimpse he had of the delightful trio was that of Chim huddled in a heap in Alma's arms, but softly and approvingly licking Mrs. Akmé's hand that encircled the waist of his mistress. For Chim, too, was giving her thanks.

" Really, it is sublimely ridiculous, and at the same time awfully touching," said Lennox to himself, as, seizing his hat and forgetting his cane, he hurried away. " I suppose— " thought he, as he rushed through the streets, half upsetting a baby-carriage and half upset by a dog that ran between his legs—" confound it," thought he, " I believe that frizzled dog is bewitched, and I am under the spell. What a beauty she is ! Heavens ! but that is a lucky dog ! I wish I were in his place. Fie, my dual,

I'm ashamed of you. I ought to laugh at the scene I've witnessed; but I can't, for dear Mrs. Akmé has the magnetism of sincerity, and you are dragged along as you protest against the absurdity. And what a lucky fellow I am to have saved that dog, that found that home, for that angel !"

Thus assenting, dissenting, protesting and affirming, Lennox Montague became that woeful bundle of contradictions, that capricious antithesis, that most unreasonable of all reasoning animals—a man in love! He did not know what was the matter with him; but he returned to his F Street den the victim of new sensations.

The two fascinating women, now seated on a low divan, talked long and earnestly in subdued, silvery tones, with Chim resting between them, all curled up in a fluffy coil, his dreamy eyes squeezed tight shut, sleeping serenely in sweetest slumber, overcome by the excess of his great happiness.

He, the hero, who, like knight-errant of old,

had gone forth to do battle with the ogre in his den, who had been victorious, and gained paradise for her whom he adored, as well as a luxurious home for himself, and a true matron's protecting care for them both.

What dreams do all those little twitching movements, watched by four loving eyes, betray?

Chim dreams of the green hills of Washington, of the lonely hours while his mistress gives her daily lessons for bread, of his sympathetic tears for her sorrows, of the lessons that made him an educated dog, of the rewards given, of the verdant meadow beside the brooklet; then the scene changes, and the terrible nightmare of the hurdy-gurdy oppresses him; he feels the weary trotting on all day, day after day, footsore, heartsore and hungry; fleas disport themselves in his unkempt hair, and torture him; he moans, for he is beaten; he shivers, for he is cold, oh, how cold! Then the street performance, the having to earn his bread by those straining leaps, tired and faint as he was.

Ah, the sun shines at last upon his blank despair, the manly youth rescues him, a loving woman shelters him, and these dawning glimpses of a brighter future now open into the glory-flooded light of reunion with her; and in the midst of his great content his senses dissolve into dreamless sleep.

Oh, Chim, when perchance mortals sink into sleep like that, they awaken revivified, having been strengthened by the elixir of life.

What a mystery is here unfolded, that *oblivion* is needed to build spent forces anew. Yet, let neither dog nor man seek to unveil the future.

Ah, Chim, not even in dreams' magic visions can you foresee the dawning glories of the rising sun !

To-day you are but a skye-terrier, but tomorrow you are to be—a pundit !

The foregoing may appear rhapsodical, but it is simply incidental to the theosophic belief of a transmigration of souls, as we shall presently realize.

The doing of a good deed, even if the motive is not flawless, brings a reward. This Mrs. Akmé experienced, as this hitherto lonely woman was comforted by the lovable Alma Aylwyn, and she felt a profound happiness to which she had long been a stranger.

These two women intuitively knew and understood that they needed each other. Which one had really gained the most? The world, the dollar-counting world, exclaims: "The gain is for the orphan girl."

Mrs. Akmé knew better how to measure the real with the unreal. She knew how little money counts, beyond the necessity of living.

How natural the situation was, after all. They had similar family traditions, with a unison of tastes and cultivation, while the contrasting differences only held them the more closely together, for the experience of the matron supplemented the inexperience of the maiden, and there were no points of dissimilarity to make discord.

And this learned woman, usually so indifferent, except as to literature, and theses, and philosophy and progress, had the deep fountains of her affections touched, and an upspringing love of this artless girl, who was henceforth to be as her very own, overshadowed in its human intensity for the moment even her enthusiasm for the wisdom-religion, and for Chim as an illustration of its creed.

At her earnest request, Alma gave the history of her life, and the story was all the more pathetic because of its simplicity.

While this recital was being made Chim slept, but as the monotone of her voice ceased, he awoke, and barked for something to eat, which suddenly reminded Mrs. Akmé of the bodily needs of her newly adopted child. Her luggage, which had been left at the station, was sent for, a tempting lunch spread before her, succeeded by a delightful drive to the Soldiers' Home, for it was one of Washington's balmy winter days. The invigorating drive was followed by a quiet dinner, and Alma's piano playing made the evening pass pleasantly. Mrs.

Akmé, although not herself a fine musician, had a cultivated ear, and could appreciate the accuracy and delicacy of Alma's touch.

Finally Mrs. Akmé took Alma herself to a beautiful room, only separated from her own by an artistic *boudoir*, which was draped in sky blue, in compliment to the skye. As they entered the charming apartment together, Mrs. Akmé embraced Alma, and said, " My dear child, this is your own room, I beg you will feel at home in it, and find it restful. It is your sanctum, for no one can grow mentally without setting apart some time each day as sacred to solitude. It is willed, my dear, that your struggle for subsistence is ended, and that our fates shall henceforth be united, but," and she hesitated, " I beg of you one favor in return for all I hope to do to make you happy."

Mrs. Akmé was always very composed, as one accustomed to society, and no formal occasion of conventional life could have embarrassed her, but she felt deeply now, and almost ashamed too, to place such stress on a slight thing, and she was visibly embarrassed as she added, " This *boudoir* that connects our rooms is his *adytum*—I wish that he should occupy it alone. Thus he will belong to us both, and—well, I beg you to teach him to share his love for you with me."

It is said reluctantly, yet truth compels the avowal : This seeming nothing that Mrs. Akmé asked in return for a luxurious home, and a loving reception in it, was really the greatest sacrifice this excellent lady could have required of her ward. Alma yearned so to have Chim to herself, to place him as he was placed in their simple room in a village boarding-house, where he used to curl himself into a downy ball, and sleep divinely. It is not the only instance where an humble home has given some real happiness in its homely comforts, that the gilded cage of a palatial mansion cannot offer.

Alma was truly and deeply grateful, and so she at once checked the nascent selfishness. " It shall be quite as you wish, dear madam," she said. Then turning to Chim, who had

stood beside her, looking from one to the other
during the course of the conversation, she said
in a tone of authority which Chim had been
trained to heed, " Here, sir, is your room, and
here you must sleep," putting him down on a
triangular blue satin-covered canopied couch,
with eider-down quilt and pillows piled up,
and snugly fitting in a corner sheltered from all
drafts. Mrs. Akmé looked on. The dog feign-
ed not to hear, and sliding off the low couch
ran into Alma's room, where he lay down on
the rug at the foot of her bed, putting his head
between his forepaws, after a way he had when
he was taking note of things around him. He
kept his weather-eye wide open, and the only
sign he gave of life was an almost imperceptible
movement of his tail. But he had to deal now
with the firm will of his trainer, and she was
not to be thus deceived. " Chim, sir!" she repeated in a severe tone of displeasure, pointing
to the next room in the direction of his bed.

The poor little creature recognized the inevitable, and straightening himself out, he

slowly and abjectly dragged himself along on
his stomach, letting his hind legs stretch out
limp. Now and then he made short pauses as
if for reprieve of the hard sentence, but finding
from the inflexible attitude of his mistress, that
he must obey, he finally reached his couch,
and with a feeble hop, as if it were an expiring
effort, he settled himself down, with a low whine.
But as Mrs. Akmé now came forward to cover
him with the quilt, he gave decided evidence
of renewed vigor, as he quickly tossed it off,
with a wicked red gleam in his angry eye.

Then Mrs. Akmé, who had perfectly meas-
ured it all, again embraced Alma as she bade
her " good-night."

" Thanks, my dear," she said, " you are good
and true."

But Chim, the little rascal, was revengeful
for once, and did his best to disturb them both,
for he had an uneasy sleep, in which he certainly did snore, at intervals twitching and
giving undoubted symptoms of heartache or
indigestion. And so naughty was he, that

once, indeed, Alma, who could not sleep that
night, caught the recreant puppy actually
sneaking into her room; but upon her decisive
" *Chim, sir!* " he guiltily slunk back.

"What did he do?" called out Mrs. Akmé,
who had also left the door of her room ajar,
and who was passing a sleepless night.

"He tried, madam, to come to me," answered Alma.

"An astonishing proof," soliloquized Mrs.
Akmé, "of the conflict of the antagonisms of
transmigration. Here we have the aura of the
pundit imprisoned in the shell of a dog. The
principles are at variance, and yet it is but a
phase of successive reincarnations."

CHAPTER V

CHIM'S DÉBUT

THE two ladies breakfasted at a late hour the next morning. Mrs. Akmé looked somewhat careworn, and Alma a trifle pale. She was a typical American beauty, this lovely wild rose, of a good old stock. In stature about medium height, *svelte*, and her movements had a willowy grace suggestive of suppleness and strength—what, indeed, might aptly be described as facile force. One felt that she was amiable enough to yield, and at the same time was firm where resistance was needed. As to her complexion, it was simply faultless; fair, and with coloring of roseate, vivid, changing tints.

Mrs. Akmé looked at her admiringly, with the thought that " beauty was captivating, but when allied with goodness, was lovable," for already had she experienced the healing power of this companionship.

Chim sat between them, none the worse for the uneasy slumbers of the past night, and quite restored to good humor over his lamb chop, as, indeed, many people are during the appreciative discussion of a satisfactory breakfast.

The butler, careful for the napery, had tucked a napkin round his neck as best he could, for Mrs. Akmé had absolutely forbidden the use of a pin as dangerous.

"This is a precaution," she said, "that heedless mothers are apt to neglect. Their babies cry because they are scratched, then they yell because, when they wriggle, the pin sticks the deeper. I know," she added, apologetically, "that it is bad form for Chim to have this napkin under his chin."

"Yet," suggested Alma, gravely, "I am told that English well-fed aldermen do it, and even the Lord Mayor of London when he dined with Whittington's cat, and Chim comes of Anglo-American stock."

"True," said Mrs. Akmé approvingly, "it is probable he was an Anglican alderman in one of his life-cycles."

"He may have been Mother Goose," said Alma laughing, not realizing the profundity of her friend's remark.

"My dear child," replied she with dignity, "the apparently incoherent recitals of this nursery book, especially these rhymes regarding animals, have a deep allegorical meaning, some of them archaic, and can be traced back to Plotinus."

Alma never having heard of Plotinus, felt her ignorance, and so very naïvely answered, "I don't know: I have so much to learn."

The most expert courtier could not have better pleased Mrs. Akmé, who knew society, was tired of its pretentious ways, and found an infinite charm in unaffected simplicity. Then the rôle of superior acquirements, thus gracefully conceded her, was to her liking.

This winter breakfast-room, in which the trio were, was cozy and had the glow of the south-

east light so cheering of a winter morning, when
Washington is irradiated by her brilliant sun.

Just then a broad, bright ray like a warm
welcome, rested on the rich abundance of the
soft brown and golden hair of the young girl,
and flitted around her figure, investing her
with a sort of diaphanous atmosphere.

"A benison has fallen upon my lonely
home," thought the matron: "this dear child
is a pleasing neophyte to instruct."

At that moment Lennox Montague's card
was handed in. Mrs. Akmé liked Lennox
very much, but she did not like being disturbed at all hours.

However, she said," Show Mr. Montague in,"
and as he entered, she said kindly yet pointed-
ly, "Good-morning, Lennox; I thought these
were your hours for church."

This little speech was perfectly understood
by the youth, and acted as a useful tonic for
the future when he was tempted to seek Alma
at other than visiting hours. The fact was,
his desire to meet Alma again had been irre-

sistible, but he had the *savoir-faire* to collect himself, and with the hurried air of a man who has no time to lose, declined the proffered chair, though it cost him a pang to do so.

"I have ventured to call at this unseasonable hour," he said affably, "wishing to find you at home, Mrs. Akmé, and to offer my services in case you need them for this evening."

"Thanks," said that lady with a twinge of self-reproach, "you are very thoughtful." She paused a moment, then added:

"I had intended writing a note to Professor Wissy-Wassy, who is to introduce Chim to our Society of Adepts, in order to acquaint him with the remarkable coincidence of the arrival of Miss Aylwyn in that connection, but if you will kindly call upon that gentleman and inform him of all the facts you will greatly oblige me."

There are some things in occultism difficult to put upon paper, and better explained in a conversational way.

Alma's mind was confused by this mode of

speech so new to her—"introduce Chim to the Society of Adepts," and "occultism," connecting Chim and herself. She began to feel as if it were all some strange hallucination, and Chim perhaps the genie that rubbed Aladdin's lamp.

Just then Chim jumped down out of his chair, pulling the napkin off, and hopped up into Alma's lap, looking in a half jealous way at Lennox who had noticed him with repressed merriment.

Almost as if divining Alma's thought, Lennox said, " Perhaps, Miss Aylwyn, Chim is good enough to mistake me for the prince of the fairy tale, and he asserts himself."

Conscious of an undefined sentiment she wished to repress, the eyes of the beautiful girl took on the hue of the deep blue sea, and her cheeks were aflame as are the glowing sunlit waves.

Lennox in his turn wondered " how much more such loveliness would upset his reason," while Chim, as if taking in the situation from his vantage-ground, glared round the table in a very spoiled way.

Suddenly his mistress, recalling the request of Mrs. Akmé, said to the dog, " Down, sir." As he did not stir she quietly arose, letting him slide to the floor. Chim would have been miserable indeed could he have known of an almost imperceptible heart-throb of his fair tyrant, which, like a shadow half-concealed, foretold that she might some day live, move, and have her being, with another object reigning supreme in her affections. Ah, Chim, thou knowest not yet how lamentably fickle is a woman's heart!

Petted children sometimes pretend to be hurt when they are not, if it is attempted to punish them, and Chim, like a spoiled child, cried when he was put down.

" Oh," said Mrs. Akmé with solicitude, " can he be hurt ? "

" Not at all hurt," replied Alma quietly; " he is only naughty," and she stooped down and gave him a smart slap.

This punishment did him good, for he stopped crying, and moved his tail in a supplicating way.

"Go back to your chair, sir," said Alma.

Chim obeyed the command. Lennox was delighted to see that much common sense left to womankind.

Ah, Chim, you were unwittingly pointing a moral, for before this day closes you are to have an apotheosis, but the foundation is laid in your first being humbled! Such are the lights and shadows of a life!

Lennox then said, "I will at once go and see the professor, who, I fancy, can be found in his study at this hour." So bidding the ladies and Chim "good morning," he went away.

After he left, Mrs. Akmé remarked to Alma, "I quite forgot to mention to you, dear, in connection with the day, that I have no formulated creed that takes me to any church. I have long ago emancipated myself from thraldom, and thought-freedom in the largest sense is what I seek. Yet I desire that others should also have the same liberty. But I fear it is now too late for any of the morning services, for I heard the church bells ring while we were at breakfast."

Alma said, "Thanks, Mrs. Akmé; unfortunately I am not a professing Christian, although I love to go to church, especially I enjoy the ceremonies of the Catholics."

"I have a friend," replied Mrs. Akmé, "who has a pew at St. Matthew's, and I will ask her if she can spare you a seat. After this, go whenever you are so inclined. And now, dear, shut Chim up in his room, or you may walk out together—do as you will; but I shall find it needful for my spirit-growth to be alone till dinner. This evening at nine o'clock the Society of Adepts will meet in my drawing-room. Chim will then be introduced, and you will greatly oblige me, dear, if you will see that the maid pays proper attention to his toilette. A perfumed bath, for instance, will be pleasant for him, and make him attractive to others."

Alma was very careful to prepare Chim for the evening, and while she was amusing herself with the intelligent little creature, who was very frisky and vivacious, she made him rehearse all of his old tricks, much wondering, while she did so, what part he was destined to play among the Adepts.

Shortly before nine o'clock Mrs. Akmé came to Chim's *boudoir* where Alma was, and they then accompanied her to the drawing-room.

The house presented a charming picture of quiet elegance, as the cheerful blaze of wood-fires, subdued by lamplight and shaded wax candles, suggested the dreaminess of contemplative thought, rather than the glare and excitement attending the usual society entertainments.

Alma thought she had never seen anything "so enchanting," and she never had, so she told Mrs. Akmé—a candid avowal that pleased that lady, for however sublimated her soul may have been, she liked the recognition of success.

Punctually at nine the Adepts arrived, who

were nine in number, including the hostess. And here let it be remarked that everything the Adepts did and said was supposed to be symbolical and to have a hidden meaning, according to the complex laws of the Secret Science.

So that, although they preferred to be left alone, yet it made little or no difference who was present of the uninitiated, inasmuch as no one could understand them.

They had the polished wit of Talleyrand, in making language conceal thought, for with them thought was the Saracenic scimitar, and words the sheath to keep the blade from rusting.

Alma, arrayed in spotless white, stood just a little back of Mrs. Akmé, holding Chim in leash by a blue ribbon, while Lennox, who had availed himself of the invitation to "come early," stood beside Alma in order to assist her, if need be, in the care of Chim, and he was dazzled by Alma's white dress, which seemed to him marvelously becoming.

That morning he had duly made known to
Professor Wissy-Wassy, in compliance with the
request of Mrs. Akmé, all that had transpired,
but to his surprise that gentleman took the
matter very coolly, merely remarking that he
had, " the night previous, when in a lucid, clair-
voyant state, been made aware of what had
taken place ! "

It seemed to Lennox, upon hearing this state-
ment, that this gentlemen was not a comfortable person to know, if he had the power, like
Asmodeus, the renowned devil on two sticks,
to inspect what people were about, without
their being at all able to protect themselves
against such ubiquitous espionage.

When all were assembled it was a most not-
able symposium !

Professor Guatama Iamblichus Wissy-Wassy,
Mahatma, and teacher of hermetic philosophy
and Orientalism, was a host in himself, enough
possibly to have purified the air of Washington
during a whole session of Congress, had that
erratic body only had the mystic sense to make

the needed appropriation for the cleaning of
the Augean stables under his direction. This
suggestion may seem irrelevant, but in it is
sufficient material for the publication, at public
expense of course, of a public document, ir-
reverently often alluded to as " Pub. Doc." for
short.

The. clear olive complexion, languid dark
eyes, and ascetic figure of the professor gave
an indefinable inkling of his leading an inner
life of concentrated contemplation, removed
from transitory, terrestrial scenes.

Had he only enwrapped his massive head in
the folds of an Oriental turban, and draped
himself in a flowing white woolen garment, the
illusion would have been enhanced.

Yet, even in a well-fitting dress-suit of Hei-
berger's make (and surprising to add, for a
dreamer, it was paid for, too), he had a strange,
weird, haggard look, which made an impression that the grave, deep, sepulchral tones of
his voice increased.

This gentleman and Mrs. Akmé were evidently the leaders who gave cohesion to the society. But Mrs. Akmé's delight was to give everybody a free lunch, and a free ride on his or her hobby.

This was what this dear lady called, "needed thought attrition" and "progress."

It has been said that many people call the act of *going* "progress," forgetting that if one goes wrong, movement becomes retrograde.

Mrs. Odic had been received as an Adept by Mrs. Akmé with some hesitation, not because she was a spiritualist, as it would have run counter to the grand idea of freedom, to forbid any one's initiation on account of their theories, but unfortunately for general society, Mrs. Odic, who was no longer young, had put her theories into vigorous practice, left her husband and their children, and was spiritually married to Augustus Odic, a wavering boy of twenty, whom she had discovered to be her soul's affinity. This startling application of a theory was very distasteful to Mrs. Akmé, who was a very proper society woman: after much hesitation, however, it was conceded that Mrs. Odic could come, unattended by her spirit-complement, which was rather unfair. But she made up for two, any day, although she was, as it were, only tolerated; one might say, " on trial " or " good behavior."

Mrs. Turvey-Topsey was a very able Christian scientist, who had published a monograph on the all-sustaining effect of the will-power, and its transcending potency over disease, which is only an expression of weakness. Her doctrines led her directly into the speculations of the Adepts; and she had no difficulty in accepting their conclusions.

Miss Featherweight held that the universal panacea for all the ills mortals fall heir to is fasting, which was alike good for flesh and spirit, and that the mind triumphed just as the body wasted. Her belief harmonized with that of the Adepts, who found no objection to her affiliation in their midst.

Dr. Mensana, who pooh-poohed at the very unprofessional opinions of both Mrs. Turvey-

Topsey and Miss Featherweight, only consented to become an Adept in such company because he expected to convert them, with the rest of the world, to his wonderful discoveries concerning the origin of microbes and the Elixir of Life. He felt that these additions to the sum of human knowledge were rather in the nature of revelations, and were destined to revolutionize the present order of things. Of course, when there was a sure prophylactic for the prevention of disease, and a life-giving fluid that would prolong existence beyond the allotted days of Methuselah, conditions must change. He had not the slightest doubt that the Mahatmas could live a thousand years in a state of perpetual youth.

General Alibi's theories of the mode of conducting war, so as to evolve out of threatened dangers a state of perpetual peace and bring about a millennium of brotherly love, he exemplified in his own proper person. He was mild, persuasive and suave, and so necessary to keep the wheels of government well oiled, that he had for many years been stationed at Washington, where he was constantly needed to explain the art of war and sit on court-martials.

He certainly was an adept at holding the scales of justice evenly balanced, without tips.

Then there was Mr. Epicene, who had governmental theories that the world's progress was retarded by the exhibition of too much masculine power, and that the vital magnetic influence should rather proceed from the female sex. He held that the best way to neutralize disturbing forces and restore the needful equipoise, was to let the women rule the state, so as to leave the men more at liberty to exercise the higher faculties of contemplation and scientific development.

Now, curiously enough, Mrs. Epicene illustrated his theory as she came in, as the ninth Adept, having, as such, a casting vote, and creating in the management of the society a preponderance of femininity.

Mrs. Epicene wore her hair short; Mr. Epi-

cene wore his hair long. She affected natty,
trim, tailor-made suits, and he liked slouchy
clothes, which, touching him nowhere, did not
distract him in **his** reveries. His features were
mild and composed, and hers pronounced and
aggressive, **so that** when they were both seated
in any company, this peculiar effect was produced, that people **were** incessantly mixing
them up, and mistaking Mister for Mrs. **and**
the one It for t'other It.

This confusion of identity caused no little
merriment outside of the circle **of** Adepts, **and**
among **the** scoffing because ignorant *Unil-*
luminated, **if a new** word can be coined to **ex-**
press that circle and sphere **of the** uninitiated.

When this assembly was seated it was indeed a goodly company, and one representing
as many divergences as the points of the com-
pass, or the emblems that do environ the
grades **of Adonhiram.**

Professor Wissy-Wassy claimed that **their**
order of Adepts was most **ancient of the an-**
cient, and could be directly traced to the very

root of the genealogical tree: even to Phaleg who was the son of Heber, whose father was the son of Arphaxad, who was the oldest son of Noah.

Therefore this society represented Shem, Cham, and Japhet.

Now when these archaical Adepts were all seated in a mystical horse-shoe shape, and Mrs. Akmé was about to ask the professor properly to introduce Chim, much to her disgust the giddy wheel of fashion rotated their way, and sent them a score or more of its votaries. Amongst the number, there came a carriage full of the interesting family of millionaires who needs must run after every new sensation, and who had left their own dinner table, asking their guests to excuse them, and amuse themselves playing billiards, while they met an engagement at Mrs. Akmé's.

So there entered Mr. La Fayette de Noo, a genial, somewhat bald-headed, oldish man, Mrs. La Fayette de Noo, of an age impossible to conjecture, Miss Marie Jeanne La Fayette de

Noo, and the young son, Mr. Marquis La Fayette de Noo, and following this family ava-
lanche, besides those already arrived, were a
western member of Congress, and a foreign
minister who was desirous of learning English
"as she is spoke," and several others who
sauntered in trusting to be entertained, and sure
anyhow of obtaining a good supper, which was
about all the cultivation of the inner man these
miserable grovelers aspired to.

At last quiet being restored, for it is impossible for any deliberative body except the House
of Representatives to effect important results
in a hubbub, Professor Wissy-Wassy stepped
upon a small raised dais in an alcove, and gave
Mrs. Akmé to understand that he was now
ready formally to present Chim.

There was a discrowned marble pedestal in
this alcove, upon which it was intended to
place the skye-terrier, during his little speech.
But Chim, who was apt to be wilful, and have
a mind of his own, finding the marble hard and
cold, at once jumped down and ran back to

Alma, taking no more heed of the Mahatmas than if he were an ordinary mortal. But Alma, with perfect tact, at this awkward juncture, quietly taking him in her arms, firmly replaced him on his undesired pinnacle, and standing back of him, she held him down in a way that made him quite understand that he was to stay where she placed him.

So, at last, without further loss of time, the Professor had cleared his throat to begin, when Mrs. La Fayette de Noo, who had been maliciously informed it was "a performance," and who was over-anxious to keep the diplomat who sat next her duly informed, tapped him on the arm and said in a distinct undertone, " The show, Monsheer, is about to begin." Whereupon she leveled a big opera glass as straight at poor Chim as if it had been a gun, when her promising son and heir, Mr. Marquis La Fayette de Noo, rose to his feet and brought his glass to bear upon Alma, exclaiming, " 'Pon honor, she's a daisy."

Lennox started, but Mrs. Akmé, who had also

heard it, put **her hand upon his** arm, **holding**
him back.   The Professor glared at the offend-
ers, and **every** Adept turned round and frowned
them down, and they accordingly subsided.
Now, amidst awful silence, **the** Professor said:
" Mahatmas **and Adepts, it is my** privilege, **in**
compliance **with** the request of our hostess and
worthy **Adept, to call** your attention **to a mar-**
velous embodiment **of the** law of successive
reincarnation.   Here is an astounding instance
of the Karmic complication, in the earth-life of
the occult being before you, at present bearing
the name of Chim.   **He** represents the Nemesis
of the previous existence **of an absolute mate-**
rialist, one whose materialism **was so gross that**
no spiritual ray could **penetrate; and it will now,**
as we have reason **to** know, require at least
one hundred centuries of cyclic changes, which
Chim is now undergoing, in order to revive the
latent spirit of **the once conscious soul.   Un-**
der this all-prevailing Karmic law, **behold this**
shell—"

" I bet any one in this **room** a thousand dollars to one, and will put the chink down, that he is a dog," vehemently interrupted Mr. La Fayette de Noo, jumping up.

"Père" (pronounced *pare*), said Miss La Fayette de Noo, who had been educated in Paris, pulling her impulsive parent down, and whispering acutely right into his unwilling ear, "shut up, and don't make a fool of yourself, as mère (pronounced *mare*) and Marquis have just done"—whereupon the père, turning very red, so effectually did "shut up" that he never spoke another word that evening.

"This *shell*," repeated the Professor, emphasizing the word, "may require one hundred thousand cycles to develop it into a Buddha, for the constantly recurring danger exists, that upon each reincarnation, some vicious element may be introduced that may cause the astral *eidolon* to disintegrate. Occultism teaches us that the element called instinct, which this very intelligent skye-terrier possesses, is a thinking principle, which we must respect. Owing to the entire loss of memory incident to successive reincarnations, we can have no accurate knowledge of the previous personal *ego* of Chim, so as to ascertain why he should at present be thus potentially ensouled in the canine physical body. Yet we have every reason to hope, that by the time he will have had one million lives—" at this, the disgusted Marquis interjected a very significant "*Bosh !*"

Lennox again started, but Mrs. Akmé, who was very pale, whispered to him, " It is intolerable, but beneath our notice."

" Yes, I say, one million lives," repeated the professor emphatically, " before he may be restored to Devatchan, and aspire, out of this state of mental bliss, finally to reach Nirvana by the time another million million cycles shall be run. The ancient sages confirm us in this opinion —Plato, Pythagoras and a procession of others. Meantime, our present duty is to treat this interesting being with respect, for I have various reasons, which I am not at liberty to divulge, for the assertion that it is my belief that at one time during his previous planes of existence he was a learned pundit, and yet, to this day, his poor phantasmal body bears some semblance of it."

At this, the prolonged constraint, the Professor's deep voice, and the chilling cold marble upon which he sat, so acted upon Chim's sensitive nerves, that he set up a loud, prolonged, most dismal howl.

This discordant sound reacted upon the super-sensitiveness of Mrs. Odic, who called out in a still louder voice, "I feel within my higher nature the dual principle and the antagonisms of the masculine and the feminine, for I was once in a previous incarnation a great warrior; then I was Cleopatra, and I also have a dreamy reminiscence, approaching to an abnormal vision, that in previous births I was an eagle."

"A real, live, American flap-doodle eagle?" asked the irrepressible Marquis.

Giving the unlucky wight a look as piercing as the talons of that bird of prey, the lady stalked up to Chim, who was now curled up in

Alma's arms, and stroking him, said, "my last incarnation," when Chim, who was not in affinity, simply scratched her, and growled, saying plainer than words, "hands off," whereupon she mentally ejaculated, "the nasty wretch," but checking herself, turned to the audience and announced that "a phantom hand beckoned her to the supper room," adding, "when the double in that dog is once separated from his present unworthy vehicle, every unpleasant remembrance, as in my own case, will be obliterated. Such is my terrestrial experience."

The professor now offered his arm to Mrs. Akmé; Lennox Montague was happy in securing Alma, who, leading Chim by his blue ribbon, went into the supper room. And Chim's phosphorescent eyes fairly gleamed as he beheld the feast.

After Mrs. Akmé had retired to her room that night, a desperate spiritual combat was hers. An understratum of common sense in her nature rebelled against the absurd consequences of theories, whose illusions were sufficiently captivating, until some attempt was made to put them into practice.

The bold statements of Mrs. Odic were too palpable when asserted as facts, for they belonged rather to the domain of philosophical speculation, and the brazen manner of the woman was repellent to her finer perceptions.

Nor had the meeting been characterized by that breadth and repose of philosophical disquisition she had expected.

It was true that the De Noo's had unexpectedly introduced a plebeian element, for which she was not prepared, which had chilled all enthusiasm.

But even this she could better overlook than the manifest great material enjoyment of the supper by the Adepts, which scandalized her. Would it not be better to disband the society and pursue her investigations under the guidance of Professor Wissy-Wassy?

CHAPTER VI

THE La Fayette de Noo family, who attended the meeting of the Adepts, must be spoken of with great respect, for they were awfully rich. It quite takes one's breath away to mention how rich they were, but millions and millions of American dollars—which are more than billions and billions of French francs, or trillions and trillions of German pfennigs—were scraped together out of an original nothing by the head of the family.

When this extraordinarily lucky man first started to " make his pile " his only capital was a pile of bricks, of which he was the strong, hefty hod-carrier.

At that time his fellows familiarly dubbed him Larry Noo, nor was he, poor man, in any way responsible for the heavy weight of name his family later on forced him to carry, as the result of their Parisian training.

That infliction was rather his misfortune than his fault.

The daughter had been called Mary Jane, after her mother, and the one boy was christened Mark, but during quite a prolonged stay in France, the ladies, preparatory to their return to America, made various changes, needed to give expression to their changed circumstances.

They knew that Larry Noo would always stick to his surname, but that was so decorated under their hands as to give it a really distinguished sound. Mr. La Fayette de Noo, Mrs. La Fayette de Noo, Miss Marie Jeanne La Fayette de Noo, and for the crowning point, Marquis (alas, poor Mark!) La Fayette de Noo. These ancestral names could be rolled out in euphonious waves of sound by flunkies, and could be appropriately illustrated by the strictest heraldic law.

It was one of those felicitous changes which

suited everybody—for the incumbents liked it, and the world had its laugh.

It was the old story, of people suddenly raised to a height, forgetting that society is sure to get accurate information as to their antecedents while they are strutting in borrowed plumage. No stupidity equals it but that of the ostrich, who, with his head craned into the sand, imagines that he has hidden his ungainly bulk of frame from view.

The talent of money-making, which is not a very high form of intellectual development, but which is, nevertheless, a peculiar gift inherent, for instance, with the Jews, is also given to a wonderful extent to many Americans.

A large number of our citizens actually do carve out princely fortunes by their own individual force, energy and sagacity, and at times, too, distribute these earnings in munificent charities.

In a country where the theory is that labor is honorable, one would suppose that the rich who have risen from the obscurity of poverty would be anxious to have the extent of their efforts appreciated, yet this is rarely the case.

Then, too, by a certain law of compensation, the very people who have amassed riches, when they aim to get a social standing, are apt to expose themselves to ridicule by their ignorance of the laws of good breeding.

And what makes their lapses in this direction almost hopeless is, that they really don't know that they don't know.

Yet the intuition of Americans is surprisingly quick, and the children of these blundering parents grow up to understand social forms, while their children often have the most refined perceptions.

This, then, is literally what is meant by the accepted tradition that it takes three generations to make a lady or a gentleman.

But now, again, the law of compensation comes in, and as we happily have no binding law of primogeniture, by the time a big fortune has been divided so many times these refined descendants are no longer rich.

Let us be thankful that among us there is no hope of permanency outside of personal effort, and no place, as in monarchical countries, for generations of drones.

But while we are taking our turn in this merry-go-round, there is nothing to prevent our laughing at those who ride on top if they make mistakes.

It is just as well, when the breeze blows strong, not to let too many streamers fly to the wind ! *Mais revenons a nos moutons.* There is no husband so indulgent as the American, and Larry Noo was no exception to the general rule.

While his wife and two children remained abroad several years he was hard at work, engaged in various enterprises, and always rolling up money with a sure judgment that never missed its aim.

His instinct, like that of the ferret, was inborn, and when he failed to unearth, it was not worth the trying.

And Larry had a talent, still rarer than

money-making—he knew when to stop, for just as he had gained life's meridian he decided to quit work and enjoy himself.

But now he was about to try something more difficult than "the rule of three" and compound interest.

Let us see how he managed.

His family had then been five years in Europe—sight-seeing, shopping, and always moving about, without knowing or caring much where they went, or what they saw, when the summons came to return home, that he had bought a big house in Washington, and wanted them in it. He had gotten in the habit of writing in a business way, and with no waste of words.

The family were "doing" Rome and planning an expedition to Palestine, when Mrs. Noo received her recall—it read as follows:

Dear Mary Jane:—

When you get this, mother, make a bee-line for home, and pack up your duds and the children along with them.

I'm tired watching the market and scooping in money, and am ready to stop and have a good time, and give a chance to the under fellow to make his pile.

I've bought a house in the capital of this biggest of nations, and I've given you credit enough with my London bankers to buy all the knick-knacks and gim-cracks, and pictures by the yard, and statuary by the foot you have a mind to.

But do be quick about it, for I'm lonesome now, and I don't wish to go to Europe, as you ask me to, for I don't care a rappee what they are doing over there, or how those fellows of noblemen are getting along in their musty palaces. Why, mother, me and you and Sis and Mark are better off than the lot of them.

Yours and yours always,

Larry.

"Sure enough," said Mrs. Noo reflectively, when she read this epistle, "Larry's losing his head to write such a long letter, but children, when pop says it, he means it, and we must hurry up home."

"I shall take my time, all the same," replied Miss, tossing her head.

But straight to Paris they went, for there was no end of selections to make, as Mrs. Noo felt quite sure they could get "nothing decent"

in America. Only yesterday she had over-
heard the Count Champsfleurs declare it was
" a land of savages ! "

One day in particular, after some hours' shopping in a certain *établissement*, the purchases
were so enormous, and so far exceeded anything in the experience of the house, that there
was a consultation at headquarters about it,
and the proprietor thought it safest to cable
very quietly to J. S. Morgan & Co., the London
bankers of these Americans as to the genuine-
ness of their credit before filling their orders.

But there is a limit to the good nature of
even an American millionaire, who perhaps
scarcely knows, himself, how much he is worth,
and when these energetic shoppers had drawn
upon a credit of some $200,000, they got a
cablegram signed " Larry."

"Come home—no more credit."

"I'm only half dressed," complained Mary
Jane.

"That's all the fashion, Sis," suggested Mark.

"I'm glad of it," said the mother, "for all this shopping business is tiresome."

The next steamer brought them to New York, but at one time it looked as if they would have to spend their first "season" at the Custom House. In fact, it required the business training of the father to extricate them from the huge mass of their luggage.

"You may thank your stars, mother," said her affectionate husband, giving his wife a hearty hug of welcome, "that the house in Washington is big enough to hold all these fixings."

"But what's up with Sis?" said he; "she's mightily changed."

"She's not foreign born'd," said his wife, "but Sis's traveled." Sure enough she was, for to send a young girl abroad with plenty of money and not much education is a sad mistake. The young lady was shocked at the plain ways of her father, and at once "made up her mind to keep him down to where he ought to be." "It is easy to see," she said to Mark, "that his rough talk will upset our gentility."

Well, they were a trio of conspirators against poor Larry; all determined "to teach him manners."

Let those who complain of restricted means remember that there is no end to the worries of the rich.

From the outset of our millionaire's trying to enjoy his gains, he was like a fish out of water. He loved his wife and children, and during all these long years had toiled and planned to place them where they were, and yet he had only brought about a state of incredible loneliness for himself.

Before his family joined him, and while he was still busy rolling up wealth, as he once fell asleep over the endless rows of figures, he could remember having dreamed that he was in a vault, about to be crushed by toppling money bags filled with silver—oh, how heavy they were!—while he could hear the sound of feasting and merriment in his palatial halls above.

Was there no premonition of his future suffer-

ings in this dream ?   And yet for genuine hospitality no one gave of his substance more
freely than he, for he was the typical American
money-spender of the riches that come easily
and go easily.

After the shock of the first meeting following their long separation, so changed did he
find them all that it was a relief to let them
hurry on to Washington and take possession
of the new home, while he remained in New
York for some ten days, to attend to ten thousand and one things.

As he saw them off in the cars, he stood in
a daze, segar in mouth, and hat slouched over
his eyes. " Where's the dear mother? (it was
his old habit to address his wife as mother);
where's my Mary Jane, who used to bounce
into my arms for kisses when I came home ?
where's my free and easy-going Mark ? Why,
they've come home from their travels as stiff
as if they'd stood under that Mt. Vesuvius I've
read about, and got covered with its lava and
stuck. Larry Noo has a great mind to throw

his money to the bottom of the sea and begin again," and as he thus spoke of himself in the third person, he laughed a bitter laugh.

Some ten days later a Washington cab drove up to a splendid house in the West End, and a tired man, holding a satchel in his hand, got out, and rang the door-bell.

It was early evening, and the mansion was ablaze with gaslights. A liveried flunkey, wearing a powdered wig, blue coat with crimson facings, knee breeches, and low shoes with silver buckles, opened the door. He bowed low, for the master was expected.

"Lord bless me!" thought Larry, somewhat taken by surprise, "this must be at least one of them foreign dooks Mary Jane wrote me about. But I'm told they're as thick as blackberries where there's a rich girl around; and he sha'n't have her, that's flat. But I'll be polite in my own house as the best of them." So thinking, he at once exclaimed:

"How do you do, sir? I beg your pardon, Mr. Dook!" shaking him effusively by both hands. "Glad to see you, hope you'll come again."

The flunkey bowed still lower, but said not a word; not even "*Mon Dieu !*" or "*Sacre !*"

"Confound the fellow," thought Larry, flushing; "has he no tongue in that big head he wags so ?"

At this moment the inner hall door opened, and the French butler in full dress suit, white cravat, white gloves, and patent leather pumps, bowed low, saying as he did so, in deferential tone, " Monsieur."

"Ho, ho," thought Larry. "There's a brace of them ; this is the French Minister for certain, who's heard that mother's just come over with a ship-load of things from Paris." So he again shook hands warmly, and was just saying, "Don't stand on ceremony," when Mary Jane, who was sweeping past in a rose-colored silk, *trainée,* catching a glimpse of what was going on, and divining the rest, made a dash for the head of the family, and too angry to speak, fairly dragged him after her, to mother's room.

As they entered Madame sat before a huge cheval-glass, enduring some last touches, or crowning frizzles to her hair, at the hands of a neat French maid, who wore a dainty cap which was Mark's admiration.

Madame looked around, and there stood her husband, actually trembling like a culprit—he who could have "made a corner," and ruled the Stock Exchange—while her daughter, as if fearful he might escape, had not relaxed her hold.

The son, hearing a movement of some sort, had stepped out of the smoking-room, where he was lounging, and followed them in.

"*Allez-en-voos*," said Madame to the maid, pointing to the door, and she went. Madame's French was mythical, peculiar, and pantomimic, but it was a luxury she would indulge in.

"Pop's disgraced the family," Sis blurted out, "and I don't care to live."

"Fudge!" said Mark, "what's the tomfoolery? The governor's all right. Let him alone, I say."

"God bless you, my boy," said Larry with a tear in his eye; that clear gray eye that may have grown dim, but never hard, counting dollars.

"Larry, what did you do?" asked his wife kindly.

"The clean thing, mother," said he honestly. "I shook hands with two foreign ministers when I came in, or leastwise one fellow may have been a dook."

"My husband!" she groaned, "we *are* a disgraced set—them's our French servants, our valleys!"

"Ha, ha," roared the son, "that's the best thing out. Bully for you, governor!" and he patted him on the shoulder approvingly.

"French be d——d!" cried Larry as he took in the situation.

"*All* our people are French in this house," said she firmly.

"Horrible! horrible!" groaned Larry, sinking into the first chair, "I shall starve outright."

"You must *polly-voos*," said she.

" Never a word of their frog-splitting palaver !" shouted he vociferously.

" I declare," interjected Mark, " this'll be the death of me."

" You'll *have* to," said mother decisively, slowly, " from now, henceforth and forever, for you've got to be a *polly-voos* your own self."

" Mother," he said seriously, "don't abuse me before the children."

" Larry," replied she, "don't take on so, but it *has* to be. This family has had a decision, and to start right from the first fundamentals in this here society, we've *got* to be born again as it were."

" Did you all get religion ? " interrogated Larry in a pitying tone.

" I shall die," giggled the son hysterically. " Did I ever expect to live and see such raring-tearing fun ? "

" You shut up," said Sis, who was recovering. " Mother, don't keep Pop on tenter-hooks."

" Out with it, then," groaned the victim.

" It's just this, Larry," she said coaxingly.

"We've all got to air new names to suit our new social atmospheres. Now don't disremember after you're told, but you are *Mr. La Fayette de Noo*."

Larry rose and stood before her solemnly. "So help me God," he asseverated, holding up his right hand, "if my mother played me true, I came into this world plain, honest, Larry Noo."

"No, you didn't," chimed all three in chorus, Mark with a merry twinkle in his eye, "we are, every mother's son of us, La Fayette de Noo's."

"The Lord help us, then, in the midst of our afflictions," ejaculated Larry devoutly. He had not felt so pious for years.

"Let me introduce my noble parents to each other," interrupted the jesting youth. "Mrs. La Fayette de Noo this is Mr. La Fayette de Noo, or, familiarly, the governor, and this is Miss Marie Jeanne La Fayette de Noo, for all she don't look it, and I am, ladies and gentlemen, Mr. Marquis La Fayette de Noo."

"It's lucky," said Larry, with a half woe-be-gone, half comical look, "that we all changed together."

"*Oui, Père*," said Sis.

"And am I a pear, too?" groaned **Larry**. "A green one, I suppose."

"Tell him, Mère," said Sis, superciliously.

"Don't call your mother names," said the indignant père.

Again the son was in roars of laughter. "It's better'n a play," said he in great glee.

"You're a fine young puppy for a French dog" said Larry approvingly, and they shook hands.

"Perhaps, guv'nor, I'm the French minister," suggested the dutiful son.

"Now, none of that," said Larry, getting red.

"But say, mother, when may a man call you 'mother,' and Mary Jane 'Sis' and this young popinjay 'Mark'? I can't forget these dear names."

Said the mother, "These names, Larry, are to be *strictly private.*"

"One more thing," added the daughter; "if Pop won't or can't talk French, at least he ought to promise, on account of the family dignity, to say nothing."

"I'd rather be deaf and dumb till doomsday," said Larry, "than wag an oily French tongue in my head."

So the family council was over.

Mr. La Fayette de Noo was made to offer his arm to Madame, and Mr. Marquis to Miss, and they dined in solemn, silent state, after which Larry Noo put on his hat, stuck his segar in his mouth and went to Welcker's, where he got all he wanted for the asking, which he never could do at home on account of the conversational language, or want of language, of the family.

Mary Jane builded better than she knew, for after this, society never suspected what a good roystering, boon-companion it had lost. Now and then, to be sure, under great excitement he forgot himself, as at Mrs. Akmé's when he had to splurt out against that brazen lie of

calling a dog "a shell."   But Sis watched this
root of the family tree, and was at hand to pull
him back behind his cruel iron mask of silence.
So senators and cabinet ministers and society,
at large admired him as a wonderful man who
was so weighed down by the fabulous fortune
he had amassed, that he was always absorbed
in thought.   He became known and spoken of
as "the silent man," and one who knew too
much, only no one could draw him out.   Well
he was wise, for there was a family secret, and
he hid it.

Yet, now and then, some spark of the old
humor glinted out, and he had his own joke,
"in spite of 'mother' and 'sis,'" and that
huge Kraken that overshadowed his life—the
family dignity.

One of these practical jokes of his came
about in this wise:

The La Fayette de Noo ladies, who "on
principle" brought everything over from
France (they were not Anglomaniacs but
Frenchmaniacs), had imported some superb

carriages, with the panels emblazoned, as Madame explained, "with their own devices."

Some days after the arrival of the *paterfamilias*, the family were about to drive out in a splendid clarence, when just as Larry Noo had one foot on the carriage-step, his attention was arrested by the heraldic delineation on the door-panel.

He stopped point-blank, and designating the object with his forefinger, inquired of Mark, "Say, what's that?"

"Get in," called out his wife, "and let the footman shut the door."

But in place of getting in he got out, and Mark encouraged him by slamming the door shut, and telling the man to mount the box, which the fellow did, of course.

"Now," said Mark, lowering his voice, "that's our coat-of-arms."

It was a device with sixteen quarterings surmounted by a cock for a crest.

"He's a fine cock," said Larry approvingly. "I suppose Sis got one of them old masters she talks about, to paint him."

The unconscionable son replied, "Just so."

"I see the **rooster**," again **interlocuted** the father, "but where's the coat-of-arms?"

"It's there, guv'nor," said Mark, "only it's painted in the background of the cock, and you can't see it."

"I can see well enough to see you're a young- cockscomb," said Larry, who felt that his son was amusing himself.

"No sir," said this incorrigible boy; "it's painted there to show that you are cock of the walk. It's called a crest."

"The crest for me is money bags," said Larry. "We'll have one full of American silver dollars and tumbling out on the crest of the cock."

Mark liked a joke any day better than even the family dignity, and it was painted in accordingly. The whole town had its laugh before the ladies de Noo noticed the addition. Since then the family have been familiarly designated as "money bags," and when one gets a nickname neither paint nor money can rub it out.

Unlike Mr. Buncombe Hereford, who happily understood the art of giving exclusive dinners, by which his aims were imperceptibly but surely reached, and his social *prestige* enhanced, the La Fayette de Noo's made the usual mistake of the *parvenu*, in at once dazzling the social mind by entertainments on a very magnificent scale.

The social conditions of Washington are so intertwined with the social-official life, and the large receptions of official magnates are so regulated by an abnormal growth, which had its origin under the Jackson dynasty, that Washington is the most hazardous of all cities which the wealth of Crœsus may choose for its exhibition.

The crushes that follow promiscuous invitations defy the limits of any building other than the Capitol.

The old residents, who dispense unceasingly the most graceful hospitality, understand where the quicksands are, and how to avoid them, and they look on the outside hurly-burly of heralded and advertised pageants with amused comment.

One goes to the window and sees the circus as it passes, but the show does not enter your house.

But these fine distinctions of the extrinsic and the intrinsic were precisely those that the La Fayette de Noo's failed to discriminate.

And then, as has been said, when one don't know, they don't know that they don't know.

With culture at a low ebb, and notions of fine manners that were original if not elevating, they read the wonderful descriptions in all the papers of what they had done, were doing, and were going to do, with unbounded delight.

Every morning they gave audience to reporters, who dilated most felicitously regarding all their movements, chronicled their gowns, their sumptuous surroundings, and, as the time drew near, described with skilled particularity their arrangements for the coming big ball.

" Money can do a heap," said Mrs. La Fayette de Noo, and it did purchase beauty of

form, and color, and contrast, and effect, all
but one lonely height which it could not reach.

It placed this family amid the enchantments
which the brain of the gifted could create and
produce, but, having done this, that was the
consummation and the limit; and this treach-
erous money-demon, having carried the De
Noo's to a pinnacle, and set them thereon before the world's gaze, could do no more.

The creative work of redeeming them from
themselves must come from a higher plane.
Then the world, being asked to look up, mock-
ingly worshiped from afar, bowed the cringing
knee, and as they did so laughed them to scorn.

The two thousand sent no regrets to their
ball, for they went to be amused.

They ate their terrapin, guzzled their seas of
champagne, and while doing so toasted them
as upstarts, and ridiculed their unpardonable
gaucheries. Oh, poverty of money! oh, deep
abasement of that wealth which is God-given
for the uses of suffering humanity! oh, desolation of worldliness, thus to reach your climax!

And oh, ineffable discourtesy of fashion ! oh, rudeness of so-called refinement ! oh, distortion of superior intelligence, to descend to the littleness of abusing that hospitality one accepts !

The Arabs do better than the spoiled circles of fashion, for, having once broken bread within the tent-door, that precinct is sacred.

All the details, even to the elaborate and profuse floral decorations were now completed for the ball of the season, and yet, such is the contrariety of the feminine fancy, Mrs. La Fayette de Noo was not content.

There was one object that she craved, and could not obtain. To explain: That evening when, in defiance of all the proprieties, the La Fayette de Noo's had left their own dinnerguests to amuse themselves as best they could, and precipitated themselves uninvited into the *salon* Mrs. Akmé was holding, Mrs. La Fayette de Noo determined, if money could do it, to own a dog like Chim.

She had been told that Mrs. Akmé belonged

to a very old family, and when she went home
that night she at once talked it over with Mary
Jane.

She said : " You see, Sis, it's the very pink
of elegance to dress in white, like that Miss
did, and hold a dog tied with a blue ribbon,
and we'll copy after that when we give our
party."

" That's so," said Sis, "only I won't wear
any such plain white gown, and no jewelry, like
she did—catch me doing it."

" We'll not fuss about the gown," said the
mother ; " but the dog we must have."

Mrs. La Fayette de Noo had been deeply
impressed that evening. She went there to
" take notes as to how gentility acted," as she
confided to Sis, and she " came home in a
muddle."

The learned jargon she had not understood
one word of, and no one could blame her for
that ; the quiet dignity of Mrs. Akmé, the sweet
simplicity of Alma, and, above all, that extraordinary dog, had their influence with her.

So she set about in earnest to try and get just such a dog. She went to Schmid's; she sent her *valet* on to explore New York. Then she cabled to London and Paris, but all in vain. Nothing could be found at all like her description. She wanted a dog that was "a shell," "that had had more lives than a cat," that "sat upright at table, drank tea, assisted to receive, and conversed."

Her cablegrams on the subject were almost as voluminous, if not so expensive, as those of our late verbal war with Chili, and, like it, without aggressive result.

When all else had failed, she bethought herself to advertise in the Washington *Star*, which the city takes.

Some kind friend suggested it, so the following advertisement appeared:

"Wanted, at Hotel La Fayette de Noo, a trained skye-terrier, like Mrs. Akmé's. The price no consideration."

. . . .

Poor Mrs. Akmé did not read the advertisements of the *Star*, although she greatly enjoyed that well-conducted paper, and her astonishment was great the next day to find her house an object of the intense interest of a motley crowd. At first she feared a fire, and sent Harman out in the street to inspect the building. The man came in smiling, but reported "all safe."

The next surprise was, that when she and Alma and Chim attempted to drive out for an airing, such a lot of loafers rushed to the doorsteps that they all three precipitately retired, taking shelter within.

"Really, Alma, I must send for the police and clear the street," she said. "I believe the world's agog."

Alma looked frightened. "Perhaps they are Mafias," she suggested, "and don't like the Adepts."

Mrs. Akmé was prudent, and she thought a moment. "We will keep within doors, to-day, dear," she said, "but let Chim amuse himself, if he can, looking out of the window, since the poor little dear must stay in."

So they let Chim look out, who got very much displeased and barked violently.

Being of an aristocratic breed, naturally he disapproved of tramps. It's queer how dogs discriminate. Later he got sleepy, and did not dine with them; in fact, they had never seen him so drowsy as he became after Harman had given him five o'clock tea.

"A wonderful creature," said Mrs. Akmé, "he looks like an opium-eater."

So he was put to bed, and they dined without him.

.   .   .   .

That evening Mrs. La Fayette de Noo, being at dinner, received a mysterious message.

She at once hurriedly arose, without thinking to excuse herself, which was a courtesy she ignored at all times. A man enveloped in a long cloak stood in the hall.

"I bring you, madame," said he, "the twin-brother of Chim. His name is the same, and so is his education. At present he sleeps from fatigue. By morning he will be all right."

Mrs. La Fayette de Noo trembled with delight. "The price?" she said, taking Chim in
her arms.

"He is priceless," answered the man," "but
to you, madame, who will treat him kindly, I
will sell him for five hundred dollars."

"*Alceste*," she called, "*le grand bourse—
vite.*"

In another moment, the maid Annette had
handed the lackey a fat *porte-monnaie*, when
the money was quickly paid the fellow, for
fear he might change his mind, Mrs. La Fayette de Noo meanwhile holding on to the
dog.

The man counted the money, and without
saying another word went away.

CHAPTER VII

CHIM'S LOSS AND WHAT CAME OF IT

MRS. AKMÉ and Alma dined alone on that
eventful day, made all the more gloomy by
the absence of Chim at the prandial feast, to
which he always added a zest; as, like most
people of fashion, he was at his best while discussing a good dinner, for it is an acknowledged fact that there is an "upper ten," and
"a four hundred" among dogs as well as in
"high life."

"I am unable," said Mrs. Akmé, "to account
for the crowd in the street to-day, who seemed
to make this house their objective point."

"It alarmed me," said Alma nervously.

"If the annoyance is repeated to-morrow,"
resumed Mrs. Akmé, "the police must be sent
for. Washington has not the disorderly mobs

of some other cities, and I cannot imagine what it means."

Had she looked in the large oval mirror that hung over an old pier-table, she would have noticed a strange smile upon the usually cynical face of Harman the butler.

But Mrs. Akmé was absorbed in painful conjectures, and Alma was really frightened.

The evening that Professor Wissy-Wassy had presented Chim in a way so astonishing to her, she had received the impression that the Adepts were a secret society with a sign-manual and symbolic language of their own, and she was apprehensive that dear Mrs. Akmé, whom she could not help but love in return for the unbounded kindness received at her hands, was, in some way unknown to herself, entangled by the machination of these odd people.

She said to herself, " Can it be the beginning of some trouble—a disturbance preluding a more serious outbreak? Can they take us for mafias ? " she asked with such an undisguised

look of dismay, that Mrs. Akmé laughed
heartily and rising from the table said, " Dear,
we will take our coffee in Chim's *boudoir*, and
see if he is yet awake."

" That was another curious thing," said Alma; " did you notice that our skye suddenly
grew drowsy ?"

" It is no wonder," responded Mrs. Akmé,
" that he was exhausted, for he got very tired
barking at that unmannerly crowd."

" The cute little dear," said Alma, " has a
great dislike for ragged or even common people, and is sure to snap at them. How much
he must have suffered when he was made the
performing dog of the organ-grinder ! What a
debt of gratitude we owe Mr. Montague, or
rather do I, dear Mrs. Akmé, for through Chim,
whom he rescued, I have found a loving mother in you."

" Do not except me," said Mrs. Akmé, " from
the grateful recognition to Lennox. He has
given me my treasures," and placing her arm
around Alma's waist, she added, " upon sec-

ond thought we will not disturb Chim, but you
will make music for me, will you not ? "

Alma was really a musician. She had in
part received her musical education at a con-
vent near Wheeling, West Virginia, where
there were two nuns, who were remarkably
gifted, and who had surprising success as
teachers. It is said that some of their pupils
were told in Europe that their method of instruction left nothing to unlearn.

After they had been forced by pecuniary
stress to leave the old Manor House, Mrs.
Aylwyn, who was at that time a very sick woman, had boarded in Wheeling and sent Alma
as a day scholar for harp and piano lessons to
these ladies. But, as we have already mentioned, after her mother's death her cousin had
sent her to another school, as he said he disapproved of convents. However, the foundation had been well laid, and Alma's talent and
industry did the rest. She had splendid *tech-
nique* and rendered Chopin and Liszt admirably, had conscientiously studied Bach's fugues

and both Beethoven and Mozart, while at times
she had even the inspiration of a composer.
But she had had sharp trials, for, being poor, she
could never buy a harp, which every one knows
is a very expensive instrument, and thus she
was deprived of a great joy and solace, as well
as of a means of livelihood. However, she
tried to overcome the pain of this deprivation
by, reflecting that, after all, the piano gave
greater scope, and that there was a wider range
of score written for its adaptations. But yet
her delight can be more readily imagined than
described, upon finding in Mrs. Akmé's music-
room a superb double-action, grand concert
harp of Brown's best make, by the side of the
fine Steinway grand upright piano.

Mrs. Akmé had cultivated musical taste and
played passably well, and it was like a glimpse
of Paradise for Alma, to be able to play and
play and play, to meet her own desires. As
they walked into the music-room together, Alma said to her friend, " My happiness with you,
dear Mrs. Akmé, is greater than I can express.

Just to think of the joy of finding this harp—a something I had so longed for, but never dared to hope I could have."

" The deprivation," said this lady, " must indeed have been torture. I rarely touch the harp any more, and I shall have greater pleasure, Alma, in hearing you, if you will accept the instrument from me."

" My friend, my generous friend," said Alma, overcome with emotion, " was ever any one so thoughtful ? "

" My dear," said Mrs. Akmé, quietly, " I am only trying to imitate a lovely, large-hearted woman in New York, one of those rare beings whom wealth has not spoiled, and whose heart, like a fragrant bud, has expanded—not dried up—under prosperity's sun."

"What did she do ? " asked Alma.

" Presented her teacher a magnificent harp," answered Mrs. Akmé, " for one thing."

" Enough," said Alma, half weeping as the rush of recollection of what such a gift would once have meant to her; "the sympathizing and appreciative heart that could do that, must be capable of diffusing happiness in all directions."

It so happened that no one came in during the evening, not even Lennox, who was the favored *habitué* among Mrs. Akmé's visitors, as he had been called out of town to attend to some business matters.

So they played several duets, Alma embracing her harp with a loving caress. It required some little time to adjust the two instruments, and after they were in accord they exhausted a varied *repertoire*.

So it was at a late hour that they entered Chim's *boudoir* and stood arm-in-arm beside his silken couch, as if the strains of melody they had evoked had united them the more closely.

A low light was dimly burning. All was still.

"Can he yet be sleeping?" whispered Mrs. Akmé, with an undefinable uneasiness.

Alma bent over the divan and uttered a little cry of surprise.

" He is gone ! " she said; " we must look for him."

Mrs. Akmé hastily raised the light and looked first—as every woman does when in search of the burglar she never finds—under the bed.

Meantime, Alma carefully searched all the nooks and corners of his and her room. The dog could not be found.

" How naughty and spoiled he has grown," said Alma, half aloud; " I do hope Mrs. Akmé will let me properly punish him."

" Yes," said Mrs. Akmé, catching at her words with a twinge of self-reproach, " I know he must, for his own good and his future status, be made to obey."

The household was now aroused, and persistent and careful search made.

At last Mrs. Akmé, when the night was far advanced, gave it up in despair.

" He is lost," she said, tearfully, " and some careless person, who has left open some door of exit, is to blame. Our Chim, allured by the beauty of the night, has wandered out. I must set a night-watch.   He will return."

Each one of the domestics was in turn questioned, but they, one and all, protested that they had been very careful.

Ah, the dismal blank! the void! Chim was gone !

Mrs. Akmé, standing beside the low, empty bed, with clasped hands, noticed that the blue satin eider-down quilt was missing. A sudden suspicion broke upon her, and she called to Alma, saying: "He is stolen ! They have stolen him !"

"Who?" asked Alma, running in from her room, looking very frightened.

"Why, some one of that crowd, of course," said she. "How indiscreet we were to let our treasure be seen from the window !"

Alma's heart sank, and she grew very faint, as she thought of the probable sufferings of Chim.

Mrs. Akmé was seated in the *boudoir* of the lost darling, absorbed in contemplation, and presently she slowly soliloquized:

"Perhaps, indeed, the Silent Brothers have removed him, his canine life-cycle having closed."

Alma shuddered, for at such times Mrs. Akmé always impressed her as one bereft of reason, and her ignorance of the terminology of the various systems, philosophies, orientalisms and theories now being discussed and even accepted by our Christian civilization, was a puzzling mystery to her.

In her perplexity, and thinking that perhaps it might console Mrs. Akmé, she said:

"My dear music teacher, Sister Eulalia, once told me that if a loss was sustained, and the aid of St. Anthony invoked, if it were for the best, the lost would be found."

Mrs. Akmé in her turn looked amazed. "Pray, Alma," she inquired, "who was this saint? was he a theurgist? I will send for Professor Wissy-Wassy in the morning and consult with him. He is very learned in occultism."

"And I," said Alma, "will try the dear sis-

ter's suggestion, for she was a very intelligent,
clear-headed woman, who received nothing upon hearsay."

"That's right, dear," said Mrs. Akmé.
"She may have been a mystic. I never reject
a thing because I don't understand it. There
is so little, if anything, indeed, one really
knows. We live in a land of dreams, and all
our studies only bring us face to face with the
unknowable."

"I suppose so," answered the young girl,
"and what you say reminds me hearing the
Sister teach, 'that it was impossible for human
reason unaided, to find absolute truth, which
must come to us as a direct gift from God—'"

"But what are the signs of having received
the gift ?" asked her friend, greatly interested.

"Pardon me," said Alma, "I am ignorant.
I can teach nothing, but I got the impression
that what they called the sacraments were
channels for the mysterious grace to operate
upon the soul, and through these divinely appointed means the gift was received."

"How very remarkable!" answered the matron. "I must confer with the Professor about it."

Then they embraced each other, and separated for the night.

In the early morning the Professor received a note from Mrs. Akmé, requesting an early visit, and saying that she would be happy to have him breakfast with her at twelve o'clock, if he could do so.

Now, the Professor was really more genial than his appearance indicated, and he burned the midnight lamp, not only as an Adept in occultism, but likewise as one skilled in the concocting of oyster and terrapin stews, and the mixing of hot, pungent punches, and other titillating compounds addressed to the lower sense of the palate, the aroma of which, penetrating the brain, often left a residuum of headache in the morning. He was essentially an orientalist, in thought and modes of non-action, but so strong are the binding ties of our surroundings, that when he did act, his habits were those of a Californian.

As the astute Marquis La Fayette de Noo ir-
reverently remarked of him, on his return
home after that *salon*, " That lantern-jawed
chap showed up great on theories."

" But," said the governor, " my son, he was
big in action with his knife and fork."

" And," added Mrs. La Fayette de Noo, " I
noticed that he was complected like a Brahman
Injun."

" P'raps," suggested Sis, " he don't know
'bout Pears' soap."

But there is no reason why these vulgar comments should be repeated, other than the contrariety of the memory that often stores away
silly things, when wise sayings are forgotten.
But one thing was certain about this scholar—
that much of the time he was absorbed in a profound contemplation of the *Ego*, or, in plain
parlance, of himself. In this he was one of
many.

Now when he received Mrs. Akmé's note, he
was just saying to his inner self, that he " would
prefer to remain quiescent, so as to amplify the

sweep of his spiritualistic vision, did not inflexible fate compel him to fall to the plane of the illusions of the day;" or, in common words, the Professor meant, that he "would rather lie in bed, but was forced to get up."

We crave pardon for such shocking vulgarization of science.

Now, for some time past, the Professor had evolved out of his thinking principle the very sensible resolution, in the near future, to propose to share his present life-cycle with Mrs. Akmé. It is true, that the vanity of vanities is the vanity of man, that surpasses all understanding. It has outlived the ages, is fed by perennial Adamic sources, is a universal law of his being, and, as a summing up, may be said to be—*Cosmic!*

It may be that Mrs. Akmé had unwittingly encouraged this decision of the Pundit, for she had lavished much time and given deferential consideration to one whom she regarded as a Mahatma, and she desired to receive illumination by the reflection of his spiritual light.

But to descend to so low a plane as to link their life destinies or karmic complications together, never once suggested itself to her.

The soul cannot gravitate downward, and hers were spiritual aspirations that tended upward.

She sought Nirvana, while he was so recreant as to suffer himself to be dominated by the animal-soul, or *Kama-rupa!*

So when he got Mrs. Akmé's note he received it as a direct reply to his own thoughts, and being given over to his own devices, he said, forgetting to express himself in an occult way:

" Ha, ha! it seems she cannot live without me. Of late I am sent for almost daily, and now it has come to such a pass that she cannot breakfast unless I am there. Although I am such a great philosopher," and here he viewed his reflection in a big mirror, " I must also be kind and considerate and spare her embarrassment. She is a widow, and of course sighs for my companionship, and, what is more to the purpose, she has a fine large house, and a handsome income to enable her to live well in it. I know this, for in the pursuit of knowledge, ha, ha! I have found it out. As to that hideous little skye-terrier and his mistress, that shilly-shally but remarkably pretty girl, her latest fad, I will, so soon as I am master of the house, make short terms with them both. They must work for a living."

Accordingly, the learned doctor hastily, but carefully, arrayed himself, and at the appointed hour made one of three at Mrs. Akmé's breakfast table.

That lady, who had perfect tact as a hostess, did not mar the pleasure of proffered hospitality by any allusion to the loss of Chim, although her guest deplored his absence, but when they rose from the table, she led the way to her study, saying to Alma as she did so, " We will excuse you, dear, as I wish to have some private conversation with the Professor."

The knees of the great Teacher fairly knocked together, he was so afraid that she was actually going to propose to him, then and there.

What arrant cowards men are! one never heard of a woman who would be alarmed if a score of men proposed to her. Of course not, for they know how to say no, with enchanting grace. And the art of a soothing refusal is a fine art.

They entered the coziest room, where Mrs. Akmé retired when she wished to be absorbed in contemplation and uninterrupted.

There are chosen spots that assist to develop thought, just as moisture and sunshine promote the growth of plants and cause their germination.

Mrs. Akmé closed the door and seated herself in a large easy chair, motioning to her companion to occupy a similar one near her.

And now at last, after this prolonged self-control the reaction came, and she became agitated as all the possibilities connected with the strange disappearance of Chim flashed upon her, and she had called to her aid the one

Master, who had traveled far and wide seeking wisdom; who had explored the dreamy orient; had seen and conversed with the Mahatmas of Thibet, and who was conversant with the lore of the Kabalist, and familiar with much that was known of the ancient Aryans.

"I have so many questions to propound, my dear Professor," she said; "I know not where to begin."

He smiled benignantly with the thought that never before had she addressed him as "dear."

"These queries," she continued, "are connected with the strange disappearance of the reincarnated Pundit Chim."

"I was aware," said he, with an expression of calm wisdom, "that he had been removed;" but mentally he simply ejaculated, "Hang the dog!"

"Why," she exclaimed, with unfeigned surprise, "did you, then, inquire about him just now at breakfast, noticing his absence?"

"Certainly I did," he replied with imperturbable repose; "do you suppose I would permit the uninitiated Miss Aylwyn to have an inkling of our secret wisdom? We of the inner section?"

"But I thought," said Mrs. Akmé, much disconcerted, "that truth was a foundation-stone of the temple of Solomon."

"Madam," he replied grandiloquently, "pardon me, but a neophyte, who is only initiated in the first degree, cannot know of the uses of symbolic language."

"True," she said, but she was not satisfied; "but since you already knew of this present phase of Chim's exit from our corporeal vision, can you not tell me if it defines in any way the doctrine of the evolution of the species?"

"Most assuredly," said he pompously.

"Oh!" said the disciple, fairly catching her breath; "and can one trace through Chim, or obtain the slightest clue that will bridge over, if only by a thread, that 'impassable chasm' between mind and matter?"

"All difficulties may be overcome," answered he. But he thought, "what an infernal curiosity women have!"

"And can even negative proofs be **given?**" she inquired, "and what is the teaching **of** esoteric philosophy on this subject?"

"A regular daughter **of** Eve," thought he. "She **must needs** pluck the apple from the tree **of** Paradise, and eat it whole forthwith, and **then be** surprised **if** she have an indigestion. **I** must impress her with the impossibility of attainment."

So, orating **very slowly, he said,** "Madam, I am pained to have to say that a long and rigorous preparation is needed before the materialized spirit can be properly prepared to receive the illumination you **desire.**"

"Preparation **of** what **kind?"** she asked, **nothing** daunted.

"Of contemplation, silence, **solitude, and** fasting;" and he mentally said, "that will deter **any** woman."

As was Mrs. Akmé's habit when deeply moved, she remained silent.

The Professor watched the effect **uneasily,** and he misconstrued her seeming **passivity into** shrinking **from the prescribed** ordeal.

" Now is the time to show her the more attractive picture of society and companionship,"
thought he.

So thinking, he suddenly wheeled his chair
nearer, and bending forward grasped her hand.

Involuntarily she recoiled from its clammy
coldness, as if a snake had touched her, but
she was actually too aghast to move.

" Now or never," was his thought, still mistaking her mood, and releasing the hand she
had involuntarily drawn back, he fell upon his
knees at her feet, and cried out:

" Give me a ray of hope, transcendent being !
It has been revealed that I cannot complete
this life-cycle without you."

Mrs. Akmé pushed back her chair so quickly
that her suitor was still kneeling as she arose
and looked down upon him.

She had never before thought of him as other
than an etherealized abstraction, but now, under
this new and revolting aspect, regarding him
upon this lower plane to which he had suddenly
sunk in her estimation, how repulsive he was !

He seemed so hideous and changed that she wondered at the infatuation that had permitted her to seek instruction from him.

Her lip curled, and she drew herself haughtily to her full height. He divined the movement, and he angrily arose, and stood before her.

"And," she said with infinite scorn in her voice, "your hope of Nirvana?" He felt that he was lost, but he could not retreat. So he answered in a husky voice: "I abandon even the hope of this glorious consummation for you."

"You are base," she said scornfully. "Your soul is weak. You have no true indwelling spirit. If the Brotherhood is of such, I must seek for truth elsewhere. You have fed me with illusions, but the magic spell is broken. Henceforth we are as strangers to each other."

So saying, she left the room, and the dazed Professor, still standing on the tiger-skin rug, a vanquished athlete on the amphitheatre of his own choosing. Alternating chagrin and rage overcame him, as he wended his way back to his bachelor apartments, cursing, not loud but deep, the ill-fated day, but above all the accursed dog, that had lured him to his ruin.

And the poor lady instantly locked herself in her room to do battle with herself. "Ah," she moaned as she walked the floor, "*Eidolons* shattered! Idealisms vanished, fallacies dissolved! I begin to see myself as others must have seen me, as one bereft of reason. And for what? For eager seeking I was given chaff; for substance, words; for progress, archaisms; for Christianity, paganism. For the sublime conception of the Holy Trinity, of the Holy of Holies filling heaven and earth with symbolic beauty, a pitiful exchange of a vague glimpse of a creative essence, which like an *Ignis-fatuus* evades the grasp, and lures the unsatisfied wretch into the final despair of utter annihilation, and I was so blinded as to accept this Nirvana for the Great Jehovah! I am as one humbled to the dust, for the lesson has been given me through the weakest of instruments— a dog was sent to abase my pride of intellect. I accept the lesson taught, and oh, be he lost or found, I shall be grateful to Chim."

CHAPTER VIII

CHIM AT THE DE NOO BALL

AT first Mrs. La Fayette de Noo was sure that it would be impossible to have any cards of invitation suitably engraved in Washington, for the stunning coming-out ball for Miss de Noo, that she was about to give.

However, in view of the loss of time incident to sending the commission to Paris, for she was not at all in favor of depending on New York, and finding out upon diligent inquiry that there were several places that could be relied on in the capital city, and in particular Brentano's, where she discovered that Mrs. Akmé, and several other ladies of the oldest families had their engraving done, she rather reluctantly, and with no end of injunctions and directions, intrusted the order to them.

How artisans and others skilled in their spe-

cialties must be annoyed and discouraged, and
amused, **too, at** the various commands **given
them in the line** of their work by rich **upstarts,
who afterward blame** them **for the** results of
their own ignorant instructions !

The card when finished was quite imposing.
Had it been tied with yellow ribbons it might
have been mistaken for that of the grand Mo-
.gul. **The** famous coat-of-arms with sixteen
quarterings (without **money** bags) **and surmounted by a** crowing cock done in **gold,** and
embossed admirably, **was all** that could be
done for Crœsus.

Yet, as Mrs. Akmé **said to Alma** when they
got their invitation : "Brentano's have done
their work all right, but the rest has **the un-
mistakable** stamp of the *parvenu*. **The device, or whatever** the nondescript **may be**
called, is in defiance of heraldic law, **and aside
from** that, ridiculous in itself, **and the extraor-**
dinary **size is** vulgarly pretentious. **It** is curious that these *nouveaux-riches* cannot attain
refine**ment**."

"It must be, of course," said Alma, "because they are somewhat upset by the great change of circumstances, and they strain after effect, so as to dazzle others."

"Only look at this superscription," said Mrs. Akmé, "addressed ' *To Mrs. Akmé and family !* ' It seems by this that we are an aggregation, Alma, and cannot be individualized. There in nothing of bad manners more grating than the overlooking, misspelling or mistaking one's name in any way."

"And yet," said Alma, "this name has a *de* prefixed, which is supposed to indicate *savoir-faire.*"

Mrs. Akmé laughed sarcastically as she said, "It is made *de* by act of legislature or act of piracy. I am told the man is plain Larry Noo. He is rich, as one sees; honest, which is remarkable, and he would be a useful and respectable citizen were it not for the antics of his wife and daughter."

"And the son?" asked Alma.

Mrs. Akmé scanned her face for an instant,

but saw the open expression of the clear blue
eyes and was satisfied.

"The son, dear, is, they say, half dude and a
good-hearted fellow, but in no wise a refined
man. I fancy that the father is the best of the
lot. He had the wit to make the money that
the family squanders."

"What a queer history," said Alma.

"Not at all, dear," replied her friend. "This
thing happens every day in our midst—so often,
indeed, that one ceases to be surprised. If you
wish an indulgent husband, my child, be sure
to marry an American."

"Oh!" exclaimed the ingenuous girl, catching her breath, with an appealing look which
plainly said, "to have marriage thus alluded
to is not pleasant." "I suppose," she said,
"you are not going to this ball?"

"I ought not to go," replied the matron quietly, "for I do not think it quite just to society or
one's own self-respect to visit people whom one
cannot but criticise. There is too much of this
sort of thing done by people of influence, and

who know better, and who are really responsible for the general tone of society. Yet by their presence at these entertainments they encourage the underbred. But for once, my dear adopted daughter, I am going, as I wish to show you all phases of the world's movement."

"Thanks; you are so considerate," replied Alma; but she could not help thinking how changed Mrs. Akmé was since the other day when the Professor had breakfasted with them. She seemed to have become so matter-of-fact; less serious and stately, perhaps, and, above all, to take such a common-sense view of things. Then, she had not used a single word that was incomprehensible to her.

Alma little dreamed that Mrs. Akmé was passing mentally through a transition state; that she was shedding her chrysalis of *isms*, and done forever with the society of Adepts.

.   .   .   .

After having acquired Chim, Mrs La Fayette de Noo was at first ecstatically happy, although her gratification was not unalloyed, as will happen with one's most longed-for pleasures, because Chim behaved in such a disagreeable way—whining and discontented—like a spoiled child of fortune.

It must be confessed that the dog was far from amiable; and, finally, one morning when she.tried to overcome his ill-humor by love, squeezing him in her arms, he snapped at her, and tore her lace handkerchief.

"Take care, now," said Marie Jeanne, in a warning tone, "that dog may have been bit, for all we know, and is going mad."

"You scare, me, Sis," said her mother turning red, and looking at the slight scratch on her hand.

"*Annette, le docteur.*"

"Oh," said the daughter, who had a very pleasant recollection of Dr. Mensana, whom she had met at Mrs. Akmé's, "I will attend to that at once myself."

Dr. Mensana received an urgent message "to come as quickly as possible," and he went

at once, although at some personal inconven-
ience, muttering to himself: " I venture to say
it's only a scratch, for women always send word
that they are dying—at least the rich ones do."

Miss de Noo received the gallant Esculapius
attired in a rose-colored silk morning gown,
which quite impressed his susceptible fancy,
and she explained to him volubly, that " Madame Mère" had a wonderful trained dog—the
twin-brother of Mrs. Akmé's, and that the
little fellow must be sick, as he had snapped
at his mistress.

Dr. Mensana was not very well pleased to
be sent for on account of a dog, but he
thought the young lady quite charming, and
besides, since the puppy was of the same litter
as Mrs. Akmé's wonderful dog, perhaps he
might be an interesting subject for scientific
investigation, and even illustrate his own theory
of microbes.

So they ascended to Madame Mère's *boudoir*, Miss de Noo herself condescending to
lead the way.

Mrs. de Noo was, likewise, very elaborately attired for the reception of the doctor, and Chim was being rocked in a canopied, lace-ruffled, satin-lined cradle, but had to be held therein, trying his best to work out. Evidently the dog was not artistic.

Marquis stood looking out of the window, his hands clasped behind his back, and his cheeks puffed out and his face actually mottled with suppressed laughter, as he now and then turned to ogle the maid, who smiled irrepressibly, but otherwise did not encourage his mirthfulness.

" *Docteur*," said madame, "we are, as you see, an afflicted family. Can you give us a prescription for a dose?"

The doctor bowed, looking round—Miss de Noo, who had him in special charge, handed him a chair, also seating herself.

"This here Sheen," the mother continued, "is the patient one. He has so far forgot hisself as to snap at me. He done it this morning, whilst I was ahugging of him, and Miss de Noo thinks he's a case of being rabies. He has a right to be well conducted, as he belongs to an old family stock, second to none in the land, being he is twins to Mrs. Akmé's performing dog, the pair of them having one and the same name. I don't like Chim for a name, but the Marquis here, says, its dog's latin for Prince Coolly-Woolly."

Hereupon Mark looked very hard out of the window, spluttering out something that sounded like—" I'll be dog-goned, if 'tain't just so."

The maid twitched and rocked the cradle so violently that Chim took the chance to jump up into the doctor's lap, who was seated near.

As he looked at him, Chim gave a quick little joyful bark, having evidently recognized him as one of Mrs. Akmé's Adepts, and doubtless hoping that he had found a friend who would take him back to Alma.

So the dog remained very quiet on his knee, giving Dr. Mensana an excellent opportunity to diagnose his case.

A careful and minute search with a powerful magnifying glass was at once made for microbes, and notwithstanding the perfumed baths, several well-defined ones were found skipping about his wee, woolly body. Then this astute physician examined the eyes of the patient, which were unusually large, and regarded him with an appealing, almost human look.

It was one of Chim's magnetic attractions, that mystic, veiled glance of his, but the doctor was not given to sentiment, and noticing the peculiar look, thought it might possibly indicate incipient cataract.

"I find," said he sententiously to the attentive group, "a complication of symptoms. There are undoubtedly some well-defined microbes, and the indications point to incipient cataract."

"It's all Greek to me," interrupted Mrs. de Noo. "What I want to know is, what ails the cur?"

"The doctor's just told you," answered her son; "it's his hair and his eyes that worries him."

"Must an operation be performed, doctor?" asked Miss De Noo apprehensively.

"Not yet, Miss," said Esculapius, smiling upon her very blandly. "Since Chim is of interest to you, I will come again and watch the case, although I must say frankly that it is the very first time during an extensive practice that I have been sent for to prescribe to one of the canine race."

"But you must give him some medicine," said Mrs. de Noo, who imagined, as people always seem to do, that if one sees a doctor there must be a disagreeable sequence.

An experienced practitioner, in such cases, will administer a bread pill to satisfy the imagination, but Dr. Mensana was an inventor, and he desired to experiment. So, taking poor Chim with a strong grip that meant business, he said, "I will give him one drop of my elixir, although I have distilled it myself, with infinite trouble, through an alembic of my own invention."

"Law!" cried Mrs. de Noo, "the French doctors never make their own medicines."

" Nor take them, either," added Marquis.

" Nor am I a pharmacist," said the doctor, irritated.

"Oh, dear doctor!" said Miss de Noo coaxingly. Dr. Mensana, addressing her with a mollified tone, said, "This elixir is my own scientific discovery, and destined to revolutionize the world," and taking out of his inner vest pocket a homœopathic vial, he held Chim's nose, and let one drop fall on his tongue.

Chim slid down to the floor, strangled, squirmed, rolled over and over on his back, bending his body bow shape, and wriggling four protesting legs in the air.

Every one fled. They scattered to the four distant corners of the room, the frightened women holding their skirts tight round their ankles, as if they had seen a mouse.

" He's gone mad!" cried the mother. " He's got a fit!" wailed her daughter. " He'll explode! it's dynamite!" shouted Mark, rubbing his hands in great glee, and making more noise than all the rest put together, for, like the stormy petrel, he was at his best in a scrimmage.

"Save yourselves!" he yelled, catching Annette round the waist. "We're being blown up."

Annette extricated herself, and walked out of the room. She was always dignified, and not at all like a flirtatious Frenchwoman.

"She's pretty as a picture," thought Mark. "I'll call her back." So he stepped out and called, "Annette, the Madame wants you." She always seemed to understand his English, and she returned.

Meantime the doctor was triumphant at the marked effect of that solitary drop. Now Chim had righted himself, but he eyed the doctor suspiciously, and well he might, with a hole burned through his tongue as big as a pin-head.

"It's a beautiful case. The animal is now rejuvenated," said Dr. Mensana, solemnly. "It is probable that if no extraneous causes intervene, he will continue to live far past the usual record of the canine race."

"You don't say so!" cried Mrs. de Noo.
"What's 'rejuntevated'?" asked she.

"Made young again," answered the doctor.

"Do you hear that, Sis? He's a doctor
worth having," bawled Mark.

The young lady blushed scarlet. "Behave
yourself, Marquis," enjoined his mother. "You
forget the family dignity. You acted shameful,
too, in that saloon of Mrs. Akmé."

"Don't I know," said the exasperating boy,
"that my great-great-great-grandfather was
Larry Noo, second cousin to—"

"Hush up," said Sis, who was recovering.
Chim was now undergoing a reaction, and,
curled up on a sofa, had gone to sleep.

"*Docteur*," said madame, pointing—she always pointed to emphasize speech—"look at
that there Sheen, he's cured! Listen how hard
he snoozes. I'm ever so much obleeged. To-
morrow night we give the tip-top ball of this
season. It won't be as select, though, as it
orter be, for we had to draw our line somewhere, and so I may say to you, *noos enter*,

we only asked the mund-demy. So we'll be glad to see you. It's Miss de Noo's debutante —coming out. Do you think the Sheen will be well enough to appear ?"

"Be sure to come, doctor," added Miss de Noo persuasively, "and you may dance with me, fourth partner. My first is Count Hoppin, my second Baron Hausgärten, my third the Chevalier Stooper."

"You see," interlocuted mamma, "Miss de Noo has to give first choice to the diplomatic corpse."

"As I'm only a doctor," said he sarcastically, "I won't mind that sort of thing in the least. Good morning."

"Now be sure to come, doctor," repeated Miss de Noo, attending him to the door.

"Sis has got a mash on that there longevity man," observed Marquis. "She'd undergo cremation to be made young again."

"For shame, Marquis," expostulated his mother, "you reflect on me."

After the doctor went away Mrs. de Noo

sent word through Annette to the parlor maid,
that she must order the butler, who must order
the footman, who must order the coachman to
come round with the clarence.

"Does Annette go too, with Chim?" asked
Mark, "for that was a pretty big order, Madame
Mére."

"*Oui*," she said.

Presently the big family carriage, drawn by
high-stepping, docked horses, covered with
heavy gold-mounted harness, and rattling
their gilded chains, rolled to the door, and
Madame, Miss, Mark, and Annette holding
Chim, got in.

Mrs. de Noo had made up her mind that
Chim should wear amber beads to strengthen
his eyes, and so she drove first to Galt's, where
a glittering amber necklace was fitted to his
neck, which Chim had the ill-taste to disap-
prove of. He nearly shook his head off trying
to get rid of it, but all to no purpose, as it was
securely clasped, and, like the shirt of Nessus,
stuck on. They then drove to Zimmerman's,

where Mrs. de Noo had been told all the upper
ten went to get their furniture.

She was rather disgusted to find a lot of old
things, but Sis assured her "the older the better;" so she began a tour of inspection, pric-
ing each thing as she went along. "How
much is that grandfather's clock, mister, and
the shovel and tongs and andirons and brass
knocker and fender and silver waiter and can-
dlesticks and snuffers and coasters and cracked
china and English glass, oh, and that dear
cute little teapot and the big samovar?"—all
in a breath, but she bought nothing. Mr.
Zimmerman, as always, was patient and
polite.

Presently she came to a corner cupboard, in
which were locked up some old Dutch silver
and an exquisite miniature on ivory. It was a
portrait of a lovely woman, framed in a gold
case set round with jewels. Mrs. de Noo,
pointing to the work of art, asked, "What's
the price?"

"That," replied Mr. Zimmerman, "is a very

costly gem.   It is said to be an Isabey, and is
the portrait of a court lady; probably a French
Marchioness."

"You don't say so!" cried she. "I wonder
if she belonged to our family of the La Fayettes?"

"It may be so," replied he; "no name was
given."

"Just what I wanted," said the lady.   The
purchase was made, and Mrs. de Noo drove
off in triumph. "Let the others, like Mrs.
Akmé," she said to Sis when they got home,
"buy up the chipsofdale, and the Saint Do-
mingos, and the corner cupsboard, but I've
got the greatest bargain he had."

"How so?" asked Sis. "I know you paid
a lot."

"It's worth it," said her mother, with a wink,
"for I've bought an ancestor, being your original first parent and greatest grandmother, the
old one of all the La Fayettes de Noos."

Now that the ancestral hall was swept and
garnished, the very next evening the mansion

was painfully ablaze with electric and gas lights, and superbly decorated with floral and other adornments, for the long-heralded ball.

The cotillion was to begin at midnight. Mrs. La Fayette de Noo and Miss La Fayette de Noo were rather fine-looking women, and held themselves well, draped in superb gowns. Could they have only posed as *silent* Galateas all would have gone well.

Miss de Noo was especially noticeable, for, as she stood beside her mother, held fast by a long silver chain that was buckled to her waist was Chim, in a decolleté blue satin tunic gaily decked with ribbons, and jeweled anklets and amber necklace. He was assisting to receive.

"He was gotten up," in common parlance, "without regard to expense!"

The guests were invited at ten, which, by tacit understanding, means eleven, when they all came in a rush.

They found the entire family drawn up in line. The *pater-familias* at first stoutly swore—

for he did swear under provocation—and offered to pay a big sum to be let off; but they all
three declared that " the family dignity was at
stake," and Mark loudest of all.

So he had to stand beside his wife, and hear
himself called by a name he abhorred, for one
hour, which seemed to him without end.

Chim was placed between the ladies, and
having been well fed previously, as also all the
family, to enable them to get through the fa-
tigues of the night, he occupied himself indif-
ferently, chewing up and fraying out, at odd
intervals of time, the Venetian lace furbelows
and flounces of Mrs. de Noo, now and then
pulling off the border of ostrich plumes from
Miss de Noo's art creation, called a gown.

Being thus intent he was quiet, and, as children often are, when not heard from, supposed
to be good.

The crush was all that the most sanguine
hostess could have desired.

It was said that one woman fainted, but she
could not have been used to routs, and should

not have come at all. The jam, the **push, the** elbowing, the squeeze, made **it brilliant. Ev-**erybody said so.

The lackeys **cried out the arrivals,** announcing misnames so fast **it** was deafening **and to-tally** bewildering.

The Washington world, old-fogy residents excepted, **has a title, and the** roll-call reminds one of the naming of creation—or, not to be so grandiose, of **the** Bonapartes under the First Empire, and that " beat all creation," as the Westerner would say.

About half-past eleven Mr. **Buncombe Here-ford shook** hands warmly **with Mr. La Fayette** de Noo.

They were well **known to each other in a** business way, **and when the two** millionaires clasped hands the stocks rose and fell again, **so it** was telegraphed in **Wall Street.**

Obscure people, who make honest gains and **never speculate, have not the very faintest** idea of what it may mean **or what might hap-**pen when big guns **go off.**

Now, Mr. Hereford, as has already been explained, was exclusive in his tastes.

He merely intended to cover a prospective point or two with Larry Noo, stay a few minutes, and slip away to a terrapin and champagne supper at Welckers.

When he shook Larry Noo's hand—both hands—he knew the honest old man must dislike him; but that made no difference to Buncombe Hereford, not the least.

The world saw the friendly meeting, and after bowing to Mrs. de Noo, and paying a quiet compliment to the young lady, he fell back, with a slight nod to Marquis—just a little back of the line, as invited exclusives do at the presidential mansion receptions.

He was a man of imposing presence, and as he stood a few steps back of Mrs. de Noo, calmly looking on, he really added greatly to the dignity of the group.

Chim was so preoccupied that he paid no attention to him.

Of course, Mr. Hereford's thoughts were

elsewhere; for how can men of untold, enormous wealth be other than absent-minded?

Soon after **the** arrival of Mr. Hereford, to Mrs. de **Noo's** great satisfaction Mrs. Akmé entered, having quite a regal aspect, **and accompanied by Alma.**

Some one, feeling quite sure that Mrs. Akmé would **not** be there, had taken that considerate pains the world often has, to tell Mrs. **de Noo** that **"of course** she need **not** expect **Mrs.** Akmé, who only attended small and select companies;" so her entrance was **a social triumph** for the hostess.

Mr. Hereford at once accosted Mrs. Akmé, as society seems to have a very quick insight **as to the** desirable acquaintances it must **cultivate.**

Like the instinct of animals, it may be called *a sixth sense.* It is cousin-german to *tact,* that indefinable essence well-bred people have.

A moment before, this aristocrat had **an air** of lofty indifference **as he** gazed **over the** heads of the crowd, doubtless **at some** higher invisible goal; but now he bowed low, and as he at once perceived that a lovely girl was with Mrs. Akmé, he advanced a step forward.

Alma's graceful bearing and gracious smile were most alluring, and the simple elegance of a perfectly fitting white muslin dress would have marked her as a woman of superior refinement.

.She wore no jewelry, no furbelows, no ribbons, only a few natural flowers, and one magnificent rose amid the heavy coils of her Grecian coiffed hair.

" She is," thought this hardened man of the world, " statuesque, classic, fresh, and delicate; ah, what a rose to pluck and wear ! "

He was hastening to beg an introduction when suddenly he saw the bound of a skye-terrier almost under his feet, as with repeated yelps of delight, he rolled over and over before the fair being, who, in her turn, utterly forgetful of her surroundings, knelt down, embracing him again and again and yet again: " Chim, Chim, darling Chim," she kept repeating.

An electric thrill ran through the crowd, for what is most appreciated, because most rare in society, was being enacted—a scene! Every one pressed forward.

Miss de Noo was utterly indignant. "Please pass on," she said, "or we shall be literally crushed."

But that was easier said than done. If Alma retreated, Chim tugged frantically at his chain.

Mark, at once taking in the situation and entirely captivated by Alma's beauty, with admirable presence of mind quietly unbuckled the chain from his sister's waist, and placed the dog in Alma's arms.

They at once retreated from the room.

"What shall we do?" whispered Alma; "it is Chim."

"I know it," said Mrs. Akmé, in deepest indignation. "But now, we can only leave him here and get out of the house as quickly as possible."

Mark took the dog and ran with him, struggling, barking, and snapping, to a remote attic room, where, removed from society, he could meditate at leisure upon the ephemeral nature and the nothingness of social prestige !

And so ended the ball for Alma, and all through the persistency of Chim.

Mr. Hereford was greatly chagrined at the unexpected turn things had taken, but he very placidly inquired of his hostess who the young lady was.

"A very pert girl," said that lady, whose temper was ruffled. "She is a niece of Mrs. Akmé."

The gentleman offered her his arm, saying it was now midnight, and that she needed a little promenade.

"You see," said Mrs. de Noo, confidentially, "they may think it's their dog, for it's one of a pair of twins, and I saw the first Chim at Mrs. Akmé's, and was determined to have one like him, and so I advertised that money was no consideration, when sure enough, a man came to me with this twin of the same name, and I bought him at a great bargain for five hundred dollars, although the man said he was worth more. This Mrs. Akmé may think he is hers, but he's no such thing. I bought the Sheen and mean to hold on to him. *Voos-comprenez?*" she added, giving his arm a pinch.

"Perfectly, madam," said that gentleman, smiling in his sinister way. "Pray, excuse me now, as I happen to have a pressing engagement."

Soon after midnight the german commenced.

The Duke di Svelto-Sveltazza led, and long will that ball be chronicled in social circles, for its peculiar and bewildering arrangements, for the favors were silken purses, and in their netted depths were pieces of money.

This was the bright, original idea of Larry Noo, who, when his wife had asked him for a check to buy favors, had said, " Nonsense, mother, give them the Simon Pure, according to their needs."

And so it was decided to distribute to the foreigners gold, to the Americans silver.

The only exception to the rule being Dr.

Mensana, to whom Miss de Noo presented a twenty-dollar gold piece.

But the Washingtonians threw their purses at the flunkeys as they passed out, and what became of the rest is as secret as the archives of the State Department.

No one knows, and, what is more, no one cares to know.

At the supper there was the placing of the court circle, and then a quick closing of the doors.

Mrs. de Noo remarked to the duke, " Not one of the Corpse is left out in the cold. I took care of that."

Dr. Mensana was smuggled in behind a screen by Miss de Noo, and as to the Americans, the descendants of the Bunker Hill men and the Cincinnati, they heard the popping of champagne corks and were cheerful.

It is probable there will never be a repetition on the same scale of a similar festivity, for the air of Washington is unfavorable to the cultivation of a continuous mushroom growth.

CHAPTER IX

CHIM AS A CONNECTING LINK

MR. BUNCOMBE HEREFORD had obtained
the desired information through the garrulity
of Mrs. Lafayette de Noo, and as that was all
he wanted, he quietly hastened away.

He met with no detention, as he had taken
the very sensible precaution in such a crowded
reception of having his footman stand at the
door with his wraps.

The engagement to meet some members of
a syndicate at a midnight supper at Welcker's
had to be met, and during this Lucullian re-
past, the various aspects of a trust, that was
not being handled in a very satisfactory way,
were discussed.

The magnificent and unscrupulous daring of
Hereford was what was needed to give its
combinations an impetus, and so, disguised by

the most formal and guarded language, the scheme of wholesale robbery was matured.

A band of bandits may plan to stop a stage-coach or a railroad train, with the tacit intention of murdering any man, woman, or child who may resist their lawlessness, and yet not expose by set forms of words their cruel designs.

Petty thieves in their turn make use of slang expressions that cast an air of bold bravado over their sneaking villanies, even among themselves.

And each and every nefarious enterprise wears its own special mask, behind which it cowers to strike the fatal blow.

And so this monstrous and iniquitous trust, whose machinations were destined to smother honest industry, destroy all hope of success for private enterprise, deprive the toiling masses of men of the well-earned fruit of their labors, then dictate to a pillaged people its own terms of enforced serfdom, this wholesale scheme of corrupt and tyrannous measures, was the Machiavellian plot of these leaders of men. As everything that Midas touched hardened into gold, so even the forms of speech among these master minds were cold, polished, molten, glittering and compact.

And no vein of sympathy for suffering humanity weakened their callous hearts; no ray of benevolence could be detected in their impassive manner; no tear of pity ever percolated through the fissureless solidity and iron strength of their resolve, but they held on their way with relentless will, never heeding the wide-spread ruin they effected.

So this evening, seemingly yielding to convivial enjoyment, with approving smiles, and well-chosen phrases, under the decorous concealments of the apt uses of words, one of those gigantic iniquities, that in its disastrous monopoly overrides freedom even in this God-chosen country, reached its culminating aims. And so these scourges of the human race parted, with the mark of Cain upon their souls.

The night was far spent, and leaning into

early dawn when Hereford retired, and in sad need of rest.

But that teeming brain, filled with vast projects, had revolted against the demands of its slave, the body, and refused to sink into the lethargy of sleep.

There was no rest for its overtaxed energies, but rather it was called upon to do battle with the accusing soul.

Doubtless, during the eternity of hell's torments, in the retrospect of the probation period of human existence, it will be clearly understood that in this life were presented successive opportunities to turn off from the broad highway that leads to ruin, into paths of peace.

And that night, when sleep was in vain courted, the memories of his past thronged upon him with heavy weight.

And first there stood before him, like a presence, that fair young orphan girl whose heart and hand he had won, and whose fortune he had used as a stepping stone, much needed at the time, to attain other ends.

But now she moaned, a jibbering lunatic, im-
mured these many years in a maniac's cell.
But was it not his cruelty that had bereft her
of reason ?   He had had the power to ruthlessly send her away, to relegate her to a
hopeless incarceration as one insane, and when
that dread doom had first overtaken her, how
had it been ?   Was reason at that time really
dethroned ?   He alone knew the cause of her
apathetic, deep-seated melancholy, which was
nursed into madness.   Had not the heartbreak
of neglect and ill usage been hers, in cruel return for trusting love ?

And what had Satan, for his trembling soul
knew the presence of its Master, although invisible to mortal vision, what had he given him ?
Naught but ashes of bitterness and presaged
torture of despair.

Pleasures fatigued him; power had a leaden
weight; the senses exacted more than the body
could grant; siren voices had lost their fascinating power to sated ears, but the tempter whispered,"There remains one gratification to seek."

The time has come to throw off the burden of a crazy wife, and, once divorced and free, find solace in the artless innocence of the beautiful girl whose captivations are so alluring. And through this enchanting companionship, a fresher, purer life will be gained.

"Of course," he soliloquized, "there can be no difficulties of real moment to overcome. Mrs. Akmé will be pleased to have her niece make so brilliant an alliance, and no inexperienced girl can resist all the inducements I can offer—and all this aside from my personal magnetism."

It was soothing at last to have had his fevered fancies turned into pleasing channels, and toward morning he fell asleep.

But with the day's stir and movement he awoke, dominated by the influence of the last wish of the night, and determined at once to use means to obtain his end.

It first occurred to him that Mrs. La Fayette de Noo had asserted that Alma should never have her dog, but he would quickly secure Chim

for his mistress, and earn her gratitude, **for he**
knew she would be grateful, **he** having witnessed the affecting scene of their unexpected meeting, and the strong love they bore **each other.**

He felt quite sure that the thief, who had for
a published compensation **been induced** to
steal Chim from **Mrs.** Akmé, would find means,
if the **temptation** was **repeated, to steal him**
once again from Mrs. de Noo.

Prompt action always, **with** Hereford, waited
as a handmaid upon resolve.   **In that** *Morning
Post*, and in that *Evening Star*, was an adver-
tisement :

Wanted.—A skye-terrier like **Mrs. La Fayette de
Noo's, for which a** most liberal price **will be paid, if
promptly procured.   Address, B. H., this office.**

These advertisements despatched, **he** recollected to have been **told** that **Mrs.** Akmé's
niece had wonderful talent both as a pianist and
harpist, and he thought it must please **her to
have an** opportunity presented for the exhibi-
tion of these accomplishments.

So an invitation was **at** once sent to Mrs.

Akmé, and to Miss Akmé, to attend a small *musicale*, the next evening at nine o'clock, at his house.   Having written these notes, he instructed his secretary to attend to all the details for such a *soirée*, reminding him that in the selection of guests, the talent to be engaged, the supper to be ordered, he must direct so that every arrangement should be faultless.

Thus having spread his meshes to catch the unwary, and feeling quite sure of success from past experience, he calmly turned his attention to the vast projects in hand, with that intense power of concentration and abstraction that marked the strength of his mental grasp, and made him always a dreaded factor in whatever he undertook.   But to revert to the previous night: Marquis La Fayette de Noo, had, as a spectator of the thrilling scene that evening of the meeting between Alma and Chim, quite lost his heart.   And it was with much emotion that he had placed the beloved little creature in the arms of his beautiful mistress, assisting her to leave his mother's crowded drawing - room,

while the pretty French maid, who had taken
a deeper hold upon his fancy than he himself was aware of, underwent a temporary
eclipse.

At the close of the ball, and toward morning
he had sought his room, the last guest, except
Dr. Mensana, having departed.

That scientist was deep in the explanation
of the theory of his Elixir of Life, to Miss La
Fayette de Noo, and she was evidently so interested in the discoverer as to be willing to
embrace the discovery.

By the time Marquis reached his chamber the
house had become quiet, and he could hear the
barking of Chim from the attic, where he had
taken him for temporary imprisonment.

So he concluded to liberate the skye from
where he was, and shut him up in the dressing-
closet attached to his bedroom. " As to myself," he thought, " I am tired enough to sleep
if a pack of hounds were let loose around me."

But Marquis was mistaken. He had yet to
learn that the sharp continuous bark of one

little dog might develop mental aberration. Being thus unexpectedly kept awake by this musical discord, his fancy again reverted to Alma, and he made up his mind to please that lovely girl at all hazards, but he was also ready to hang the dog rather than spend another night within ear-shot.

Thinking over the situation, a masterly course of action was decided upon. It was evident that the dog was Alma's, and no less so, that his mother, by her inconsiderate advertisement, must have unwittingly induced some one to steal him from her. This idea as it flashed upon him, greatly tickled his fancy, and he grew very hilarious at the mere conceit as he said to himself, "It's the best thing out: mother has paid five hundred dollars to some thief who has stolen the dog for her, and Sis had the beast buckled to her waist at the ball!" Thereupon the youth laughed so long and so loud that his father came to the door, thinking he had lost his senses.

" What's up now, Mark ? " he said. " Let up

and give a man a chance to rest, will **you**?
I've not had one wink of sleep this night, although I went to my room at one **o'clock**, and
took a hot milk punch, but the infernal hulla-
baloo all over this house would have waked the
dead. Then, just as all was still, the howling
of that horrid **dog** began."

"I've been kept awake, **too**," said the son.

"**Suppose we** choke the wretch or drown
him," suggested Larry Noo. "Mother need
never be the wiser."

"We can't have that pleasure, **governor**,"
answered Mark, "because he **ain't ours to choke**
or drown: mother bought him of a thief who
stole him."

"You don't say so!" gasped honest **Larry**,
his face turning purple mottled, **as if he were**
about to have an apoplectic fit.

"**But I** do say so," reiterated the youngster,
who of all things enjoyed "working up people,"
as he called it.

His father gasped **and looked beseechingly.**

"**You** see, governor," continued his son,

"that dog really belongs to that handsome niece of Mrs. Akmé. Mother, after that night we went there, fussed to get a performing dog like him, and bought him at a big price."

"I see," said the father, looking much relieved. "But how to go about it? Your mother has the grit of Julius Cæsar and she says she means to hold on to the dog."

"It's easy enough managed," said the son. "I'll make Annette get me the quilt he came wrapped in, and I'll cover up his head so as to smother his yelps, and take him back to Mrs. Akmé myself."

"And you may take a father's blessing with him," added the delighted Larry Noo, as he went back to his room vastly pleased.

"And I," said Mark to himself, "will kill two birds with one stone, for when I give that lovely girl her dog I'll just ask her to take me too, thrown in."

Mrs. Akmé and Alma had just risen from a ten o'clock breakfast, where they had loitered somewhat, talking over, under its various as-

pects, the affair of Chim's captivity, a matter
which was at the same time being freely commented upon at half the breakfast tables of the
élite, or rather the town, for every one was at
the ball. It is curious anyhow to listen to the
critical comments made by society upon the
entertainments they give each other, where
any hostess may deem herself fortunate to escape; as it would seem to have passed into an
unwritten law of the code of fashion—that if
everything is in faultless taste it may be accepted in silence, but that the slightest infringe-
ment of the laws of etiquette is not to be for-
given. Thus, the assumptions, pretentions
and underbred ways of the La Fayette de
Noos afforded so much merriment that, in a
manner quite unsuspected by themselves, they
became public benefactors.

"I never before understood," said Alma,
"how really absurd a crush is. I can now
comprehend why well - bred people avoid
them."

"The only persons whom they genuinely

please," said Mrs. Akmé, "are those outsiders who never in any other way meet the exclusives, and yet these respectable citizens should rather resent the contact, for the spoiled children of fashion know how to be unmercifully rude to all others than their own clique."

"It is a pity," sighed Alma, remembering her own recent struggle with a pitiless world, "that money enough to have endowed a house for homeless girls should have been, as it were, squandered without results."

"Not exactly that, dear," said Mrs. Akmé; "the large sums spent in the ball of last night and similar displays are after all divided among many tradespeople, who in turn employ others. This, dear, is a sort of question of political economy."

"And of private extravagance," added Alma, laughing.

"But to revert to Chim," said Mrs. Akmé, ringing for a servant. "I will order my carriage, and see if Lennox Montague has returned, and consult him about the best way to get

the dear little creature back—for, ridiculous as
it is, there is a legal aspect in his detention."

"Has Mr. Montague been out of town?" inquired Alma in a hesitating voice, that indicated some feeling, for she had been rather
hurt by his prolonged absence, but felt too
timid to ask about him.

Mrs. Akmé was a very quick observer naturally, and her long society training had aided
her perceptions, and she at once noticed the
slight tremor in Alma's usually calm voice,
but she replied in a nonchalant way:

"Yes, dear; I thought you knew that Lennox
had been called out of town on some important
business. Had the dear boy been here we
would doubtless have seen him daily, for, young
as he is, I quite lean upon his business perceptions for advice. Then, I loved his mother,
which is a strong tie."

Alma sighed with the sad thoughts of the
past; and she passed on into the music-room
for a long practice, and Mrs. Akmé went to
her own room to get ready for the drive.

They had scarcely separated, and Alma was trying something new for the piano, when the door was quietly pushed open, and Chim bounded in.

There was a rapturous greeting, and an exclamation of, " Ah, Chim, did you run away?"

" Not at all Miss," said Mr. Marquis La Fayette de Noo, as he followed the terrier, unannounced, hat in hand, and speaking right out in his natural, frank way, " I have brought this dog back to you." He looked so pleased, and manly, too, as he stood there, that as Alma came forward to shake hands in her unaffected way, and thank him warmly, she thought him positively handsome. She had really scarcely noticed him before, but now she said to herself: " He is a nice fellow, and so thoughtful and kind."

" Excuse me a moment," she said, "and I will go and let Mrs. Akmé know of your considerate attention, for she, too, will, I am sure, desire to thank you."

" Please don't," said the young man, twirling

his hat round on the top of his cane. "I—I— would rather have *you* thank me." Alma sat down blushing, for there was that in his voice and manner that to her quick insight betrayed him.

They were both embarrassed, and Chim came to the rescue, filling up an awkward pause. It was amusing to see him smell each separate thing in that room, then inspect the apartment, with a careful gravity of proprietorship, as if to satisfy himself that all was right.

Being evidently satisfied, he ended his tour of investigation by jumping up into Alma's lap, whereat the two spectators laughed a little, and Chim laughed.

"First," said the gentleman, clearing his throat, "I beg that you and Mrs. Akmé will not misjudge my mother. It is only fair to her to say that she honestly believes the dog to be hers; and I have brought him to you without her knowledge, having sort of kidnapped the little fellow."

Alma involuntarily gave a slight start.

" You see, Miss Akmé," he commenced—

"Aylwyn," said she, quietly correcting him.

" Beg pardon, Miss Aylwyn," said Mark, again quite confused. " I was told that you were a Miss Akmé."

She bowed stiffly. Poor Mark had unconsciously committed a *faux-pas* by the use of that terrible generic " a."

There was a momentary silence; and the maladroit boy resumed, " You see, Miss, mother advertised for a dog like Mrs. Akmé's, and a man brought her Chim, to whom she paid five hundred dollars, and she really thinks he is hers by right of purchase."

" I understand perfectly," said Alma, to whom this avowal was a revelation that at once explained the crowd before the house that day, and the subsequent stealing of the dog—only it was rather uncomfortable to think of any thief having had such ready access to the house.

" The explanation is very satisfactory," said she, after a moment's pause, during which all these mental suggestions made things clear to her, and she added, "We shall always be grateful to you, but, after all, it is very embarrassing."

"Oh, not at all," replied he. "Chim was stolen from you, bought by mother, and I've **stolen him in turn from her,** to keep the ball rolling. It's clear fun anyhow."

And they both laughed, leaving any ethical **law involved to the** moral philosophers.

Now they were on good terms, and Mark, being more at his ease, said to himself, "**This is** your chance." So, drawing his chair a little nearer, as rustics are wont to do, he said, **bravely** enough :

"**My** dear **Miss** Aylwyn, I captured Chim, but **you** have captured me : it's a perfect **rout,** bag and baggage. You have your dog; can't you love me a little for his sake ? "

It was such a queer confession, and struck Alma as being so ludicrous, and yet this was the first time any man had ever asked her love in a downright way, and she fel**t a sort of grati**tude at being loved.

" How very odd it is," thought she, " that

through Chim **I** should have my first offer **of** marriage, and it may be my last, **for all I know,**" she said to herself, but she could not deceive her dual, who whispered back, " There will **be** one other through Chim."

So, giving **Chim** just a **little caress, which** must have been **very** aggravating to the poor **lover,** that it was not bestowed upon him, she answered with charming candor,

" **You** shall ever be my dear **friend,** indeed you shall; **we will** be the best of friends, **for I** *love* my dog, and I really *like* **you.**"

And just at this bewildering moment Chim, who had been listening attentively, leaped down from Alma's lap, as he barked a welcome **to Mrs.** Akmé.

But Mr. Marquis La Fayette **de Noo,** who **was smart enough to** feel keenly all that the **in-vidious discrimination of Alma implied,** hurried-**ly bowed** himself out, **and drove** rapidly away.

As the youth threw himself in rather a dis-gusted mood in **the** coupé, **he soliloquized in this wise :** " **She** certainly is **a raring-tearing** beauty, but she makes a man half afraid of her with her look of a queen. Yes, if such a woman would only smile on a man, he could lose his senses easy, and even, perhaps at first, play second fiddle to an ugly dog. But as to my taste, when it comes to loving a woman who knows your worth, and having a real jolly life of it— give me Annette any day, that is, if the pretty creature would have me, for I'm learning that women are worse riddles than Chinese puzzles."

Ah, had the whispering winds only brought to the ears of Mrs. La Layette de Noo this thought of her promising son and heir, in defiance of all family dignity, she would have set up a howl far more heartbreaking than that with which he was saluted when he returned Chimless.

But the " governor," as his son called him, quietly and surreptitiously slipped a fat check in his hand, in grateful recognition of the riddance.

And to add to the intense discomfort that the ill-humor of the ladies brought upon the La Fayette de Noo family, during all of the next day, and even on the succeeding one, the pavement, street, and carriage-way, in front of their splendid mansion, were most unpleasantly occupied by a motley concourse of persistent loafers, who passed their time in gazing up at the windows.

" *Vrayment*," said Mrs. La Fayette de Noo, " I shall have to go right straight back to Paris to live there for good, where I can be overseen night and day by a polite police, who will keep this public gaze from being troublesome."

And Miss Marie Jeanne tossed her head, and remarked—"America is such a savage country." And Larry Noo suggested, that "the rogues expected, and perhaps are waiting for a free lunch after the all-fired racket of that ball."

And Marquis La Fayette de Noo, stealing a glance at Annette for approval, remarked, "Anyhow the company outside make things lively, and I like it."

But not one of them had read the advertisements of the Washington *Post*, or the *Evening Star*, or they would have known better.

When Mrs. Akmé had so opportunely disturbed the *tête-à-tête* of the two young people, she had just received a charmingly written little note from Mr. Hereford, requesting the pleasure of her company, and that of her niece, Miss Akmé, to a small *musicale* at his house the next evening; and the invitation was accompanied by a superb basket of La France roses, which he begged she would accept as a slight expression of his great pleasure at the renewal of an acquaintance which had always been so agreeably remembered by him.

Mrs. Akmé had intended reading the note to Alma when she came in the room, but amidst the excitement of finding Chim, and the amused astonishment of hearing what had just happened, she quite forgot to mention about Mr. Hereford's note or flowers.

For Alma repeated the whole scene to her in the most animated and inimitable manner, with the same conscientious exactitude with which she would have confided a secret to her own dear mother.

Lennox Montague was a welcome guest that evening, and, as he had a fine voice, and Alma played accompaniments with great taste, the trio enjoyed a feast of music, and as he was going away Mrs. Akmé asked him to dine with them the next day, and be their escort to a *musicale* to which they were invited by an old acquaintance.

"And I, too, have received an invitation," said he. "I suppose, Mrs. Akmé, you allude to the syndicate magnate. I shall be so happy to dine with you, and so honored to be your escort."

And so it was arranged for the next evening to the common satisfaction of the little party.

CHAPTER X

CHIM'S THIRD ADVENTURE

STRANGELY enough, Alma found herself a
guest in the house of Mr. Hereford, without
knowing the name of her host. She had heard
Lennox allude to him as "a syndicate magnate," without having her interest awakened
in the least as to who or what he was. It was
evident that she lacked the world's appreciative training.

And it happened that Mrs. Akmé, who was
rather disposed to be punctilious in all matters
of form, and who understood conventional
rules, had quite overlooked mentioning the
name of their distinguished amphitryon. This
seeming inadvertence on her part rather arose
from the fact that he was a man of such marked
social distinction that there was the implied

238

supposition that every one knew who he was,
or, at the very least, his name.

And so, by a fortuitous combination of circumstances, they met, really without introduction. Mr. Hereford having been informed that
Alma was Miss Akmé, had bowed to her without repeating her name.

Then Alma accompanied Mrs. Akmé as her
adopted daughter everywhere, being well received, indeed welcomed, wherever she went,
and she had such implicit confidence in her
beloved chaperon, that in the number of their
social engagements, and the ever increasing
circle of new acquaintances, at times she became quite perplexed as to where to place
people. And no wonder, for this is a cultivated talent, the result of both training and
experience, and is often then not acquired.

The music-room had good acoustic qualities, and was pleasantly filled with genial, cultivated people, who knew each other, and all
the arrangements were charming.

Never, since her dear mother's death, had

Alma been **so radiantly** happy as on that evening, and happiness makes even the homely attractive. The beautiful girl did **not** stop to
analyze her feelings and inquire **of** herself **why**
the presence **of** Lennox Montague **brought
her** so much content, except, perhaps, **that it
seemed so clear to** them both that **they en-**
joyed **everything** with an appreciation **that**
was perfectly delightful.

When these ladies arrived with their **hand-**
some young escort, there was **a** momentary
threatening glance of Mr. Hereford's eye, **succeeded** instantly by a forced smile.

"**It is very** displeasing," he thought, "**to
have Miss** Akmé escorted by this presumptuous
boy, but I can make short **work of this obsta-**
cle," and he at once made **a mental** note to
make sure and crush the prospects, if he had
any, of this rising young attorney.

But this displeasure of Mr. Hereford was
quite unnoted **by** Alma, who **had not a special**
gift of mind-reading, so that **it cast no shadow
over** her enjoyment. One is assuredly happier

to be in blissful ignorance of invisible dangers, for the world presents to view quite enough that is disagreeable in its own time to combat.

Just now Alma's cup of pleasure was effervescing. Chim had been returned, and that anxiety was at an end, and she loved music.

As the evening progressed, her musical talent was again and again applauded.

Although some professional talent had been engaged to guard against failure, yet the excellent taste of the host desired the *soirée* to have the effect of an impromptu evening, and the adaptation of tastes had been so carefully considered, that the result was successful.

The company was an informal one with social and artistic elements happily combined, but the one feature of the occasion that Mr. Hereford intended was, that there should be an ovation to Alma, without any apparent preconcerted attempt in that direction.

Under his skilful manipulation, the *musicale* was so arranged as effectively to display her gifts. And, absorbed in the strains of harmony, she was unconscious of herself, which was the glorious thing about it.

She at first played a duet with Mrs. Akmé, which was a happy thought to give her courage until her enthusiasm was aroused.

After a time she gave an accompaniment for Lennox with much taste and feeling, which was something Mrs. Akmé suggested, and not at all in Mr. Hereford's programme, for even he could not control fate.

Then came a harp and piano concerted piece, which led to a request for a harp solo, which was rendered with an exquisite grace that elicited an outburst of *encores*.

"Well, my child," said Mrs. Akmé to her, *sotto voce*, "your triumph has been complete."

"And I dare not give expression to my feelings," added Lennox, in a low voice.

"And I," said Alma, artlessly, "have enjoyed every instant."

"And caused others still greater happiness," said the host, regarding her with an open admiration that went to the heart of Lennox like a dagger, as he felt how slight were his chances when coping with such a rival.

At this moment, Mr. Hereford presented to Alma an inoffensive dude whom he had selected to take her in to supper, and offered his own arm to Mrs. Akmé.

He knew, with a glance of triumph, that his rival was checkmated for once.

. " Ha, ha," chuckled he internally, " you are but feeling the first breath of the winter of your discontent, vain youth !   Before Hereford shall have done, you will be crushed between the upper and nether millstone of his wrath."

But could the magnate have seen the scornful look that Alma cast upon the hapless creature whose arm she had barely touched, and glanced back to see her, with a gracious inclination of her head, call Lennox to her side, he would not have been so triumphant.

For as Lennox joined them, Alma said with her sweetest smile, " Let me for once be a belle, Mr. Montague, and have two attendants."

And Lennox once again murmured, " I can-

not find words, Miss Aylwyn, to tell you the
gratitude of my heart."

At this moment, Mrs. Akmé saw Lennox,
and nodded to him to come to her. As he did
so, she said to Mr. Hereford, " I wish to com-
mend specially to your kindest consideration
the son of your and my old friend, Ysolde
Lennox."

A new light flashed upon Hereford, a new
reason for hating the boy, for he was the son
of a woman he had once loved, or thought he
loved, and, what was more to him, her discard-
ed suitor. " Now, I have," he thought, " every
reason to hate the fellow ; and he has her
beauty. I could not at first discover the link
of old association. Yes, Ysolde, you shall,
through me, act as a Nemesis for your own
child."

And thus, as the fury of revenge was raging
in his soul, he stood cold as Parian marble and
erect, and, casting an indifferent look at the
young man said, as if trying to recall an absolutely forgotten acquaintance, " Ysolde Len-

nox, **madam ?** pardon the defective memory of one who has been **perhaps** overtaxed, but I cannot remember the name," and he turned to offer Mrs. Akmé his arm to show her a fine painting, " **brought** from the old homestead," he said.

But Mrs. Akmé knew the world, and was not deceived. " Of course he remembers Ysolde," she thought; " I will cut him too;" and so she replied, with an air of fatigue: " **This** charming evening that you have given us, **Mr. Hereford,** reminds me of an absolutely well-dressed person—*there are no salient points.*"

They exchanged glances, and disliked each other.

Mrs. Akmé, who knew there was no stab so keen as that veiled by a compliment, turned to **look for Alma, but she** had left the supper-room; so, saying with **frigid** courtesy to Mr. Hereford, " I cannot longer **claim** your valuable time as host—I will take the arm of my young friend," she deliberately **left** him, and seeking Lennox, **who stood as** one momenta-

rily dazed by the cool insolence of **his host,**
she said, playfully, " Lennox, pray take **care**
of me."

After Mrs. Akmé had called Lennox away
from Alma, **she was so** insufferably **bored by**
her attendant that she begged him to **conduct
her to the library, and** then had the tact to
suggest **that he would join two of** his friends
of whom he **had** caught a glimpse in the supper-room.

This was in every way an agreeable suggestion to the vapid boy, who sauntered his mean-
dering way back to the supper-table, where he
found **two** others like unto himself; and there
the **three stood in a line, to be** waited **on,** for
an indefinite length of time, each one adorned
with a similar cascade of roses for a flourishing
boutonnière, each **one** raising **his** wine-glass
feebly to his lips from a seemingly dislocated
shoulder-blade, each one equally limp in the
legs, each one hoiding precisely the same Del-
sartian pose, and there they **stood and** stand
in other drawing-rooms, and **at other** supper-

tables to this day—three dudes with but one
single aim; three heads with but one single
thought.

The reaction of the tension of continuous
musical effort caused Alma to feel somewhat
fatigued, and the momentary solitude was very
grateful to her as she stood beside a wide-
throated open fireplace.

· There was a something in the crackling
blaze of the burning logs, in the quaint aspect
of the huge burnished andirons upon which the
wood rested, that reminded her of the merry
days of her petted babyhood and early childhood in the dear old Manor House of her
grandfather.

Over just such a fireplace hung a portrait of
her grandmother, and covering the mantel was
a rich piece of embroidery, a long scarf of oriental pattern, upon which rested those wonderful bronzes, the three musical devils, before which she used to stand aghast, shivering,
and whose images were so often dwelt upon in
memory.

There are moments when the closed cells of reminiscence seem suddenly to expand, **and** we view, as in a well-defined vista, the long succession of events that had apparently faded from our mortal ken.

So subtle are the springs that open to our sight **the** hitherto closed pictures of the past, that often **what** would seem to be the merest nothing is the needed link of the broken chain.

Ah, why should her gentle mother have had to bear the keen anguish of the **loss of** that dear old home? How cruel that merciless, grasping cousin had been to **sell it, as** he **said,** for delinquent taxes, and then, oh, shame! **buy it for** himself! **and it** was, after all, such a mere nothing to him out of his great **abundance.**

Her mother had died broken-hearted, without understanding where to place the wrong, **but** now she knew they had been needlessly sacrificed. Had not the **good old friend in** Washington, who was so generous **to her,** told **her so?**

And out of all these bitter, bitter recollections came once again a strong desire to repossess that dearest of homes. Would this happiness ever be hers?

With this yearning wish uppermost in her agitated heart she unconsciously raised her eyes as if to ask kind heaven to right this wrong, and met, looking into hers, as in the baby days, the responsive eyes of the same picture. She started, as if in fear of some optical illusion, only to see reproduced the entire vision so indelibly imprinted on memory's tablets.

There it all was—the rare old lambrequin, the three weird bronze figures writhing in their endless torture—yes, the mild, tender countenance of the beautiful grandmother.

"Have I quite lost my reason?" she asked herself, pressing her throbbing temples with both hands. "No, no, this is no mental hallucination, for clearer and clearer does the vision recall the grouping of that scene."

And now she leaned heavily for support

against the mantel, as pained and busy thought
retraced a thousand, thousand things that clus-
tered round the awakened memory.

"My harp stands mute," thought Alma, "until the living touch sweeps o'er its chords, and
so my heart-strings quiver under the magic
wand of this once familiar scene."

It did not suit Buncombe Hereford's ulterior
aims to take offense at Mrs. Akmé's caprice,.
and so he used his freedom to look for her
lovely ward, and, pausing several times to exchange a few words with a guest, he finally caught
a glimpse of her in the still unoccupied library.

He was screened by the heavy folds of the
silken portière, as he stood in the doorway.
"What an exquisite picture of innocence!"
thought he, as he watched her for a moment,
"or, rather, the pose of a model for some work
of classic art," he added, with a half sneer.
"Yet, be it unaffected artlessness, or posing
for effect, which is more likely, she is beautiful."

Her white muslin dress was closed at the
throat, and edged with soft Valenciennes lace,

and her shapely arms were uncovered except
by a fall of lace, which was looped up by two
strands of pearls, heirlooms that her mother
never would part with.

But the attention and the curiosity of this
keen analyst of character were specially arrested by her dreamy, rapt, and sad expression.

"This incomparably lovely woman," thought
he, "has a history, for no mere spoiled girl of
fashion ever had such an abstracted air."

So thinking, he stepped forward and accosted
her with that exceeding courtliness he knew
so well how to assume.

"May I dare," he inquired, "to disturb a
reverie?"

She started, then recollecting herself, replied:
"It is true; memory has been busy. I cannot explain it, but this portrait, these bronzes,
the drapery, even the fireplace, reproduce a
familiar and a well-loved scene of my early
life; it is," she added, somewhat agitated, "a
mysterious illusion I cannot dispel."

"A refrain of what, fair poet?" asked he.

"A reminder," she said, " of my childhood's home—of my dear grandfather's **house.**"

"That is very strange," said he, **somewhat** moved, "for that which interests you as rem- **iniscent is** an exact reproduction, transferred from an old Virginia home, to give me pleasure **here.**"

"Tell me about the homestead," she said.

"With pleasure," he replied with a sudden pang of self-reproach; "**it** was in its day a famous old place and the seat of generous hos- pitality. The portrait was of my aunt, its mis- **tress. Does it** remind you of a family picture, Miss Akmé?"

During this recital Alma had become more and more agitated, but she simply said:

"I am not Miss Akmé; my name is **Alma** Aylwyn."

And prompt as **a** thought of Lucifer, the father of lies, came the response of this de- stroyer of homes, as he exclaimed **with a rap-** turous manner:

"And I, my darling ward, am your loving

cousin, Buncombe Hereford.   I have sought
for you in vain, and have mourned you as one
lost."

"And what of that letter?" asked Alma,
with a withering air of disdain.

"What letter?" he asked, assuming the tranquillity of innocence. "I was about to seek you
to ask you, as I do now, to take your proper
place as my near relative, and preside over my
establishment here, when I learned you had
gone, without leaving a trace."

"And that cruel letter you wrote me?" reiterated Alma.

Mr. Hereford calmly replied: "I know not,
my dear child, to what you allude. No man
in my commanding position is without enemies.
If you ever received anything derogatory to
me in any way, purporting to come from me, I
can only say it was forgery. Your proper place
is under my continuous protection, and not as
the recipient of charity at the hands of a
stranger, as must be Mrs. Akmé."

At this moment Mrs. Akmé and Lennox

approached, and Alma at once besought her imploringly: "Do take me home with you quickly, for I am very, very ill."

"I will myself conduct you to the carriage," said her cousin, drawing her cold hand within his arm, and as he lifted her in he whispered: "My dearest little cousin; of course you will soon return to preside over my lonely home."

And he was careful that Lennox should hear the first two words, "my dearest," which had also not escaped the quick ear of Mrs. Akmé.

Lennox Montague, cut to the heart by this deadly thrust, and with raging tumult of the brain, threw himself into the carriage, escorting the ladies home in silence, a silence unbroken either by Mrs. Akmé or Alma; for the one was absorbed by too many conflicting emotions for words, and the poor young girl felt really ill.

.   .   .   .

By midnight the last guest invited to this charming *musicale* had departed, and the accomplished host, relieved to be set free from

his self-imposed duties, was about retiring to
his room, when his secretary, whom he made
a sort of *factotum* for all matters that required
special skill in the handling, came to him and
said:

"There is a man, sir, in the servants' hall,
who awaits your pleasure for the past hour, and
he has a bundle wrapped in his arms that I
fancy is a sleeping dog."

"All right," said the magnate, "telephone
at once for the special detective who has this
matter in charge; detain the man until he ar-
rives, and then let me know."

Some ten minutes later the secretary announced the presence of the officer sent for,
whereupon Mr. Hereford said, "Be quick about
it, and bring the fellow in."

In a moment a man was ushered in, with
Chim fast asleep, and the terrier was very com-
fortably wrapped in the eider-down satin quilt;
although from the rather hard breathing and
deep sleep it was evident he had been drugged.

"What is it you wish, fellow?" asked the

master of the house, with a very severe aspect, which at once cowed the trembling man.

"I bring you, sir," said he, "such **a dog as** you advertised for; a twin-brother of the one Mrs. La Fayette de **Noo** has, and he answers to the same name, Chim."

"**And** your price?" asked the purchaser; "and **be quick about it;** I have no time to waste over a **dog**."

"Mrs. La Fayette de Noo gave five hundred dollars for her dog," answered the man rather hurriedly, "and although this is a superior ani-**mal in** every way, you may have him **at the** same price, sir."

Mr. Hereford pressed the button on **his table**, and the secretary entered.

"Give this man," said he, "five hundred dollars, which is the sum he asks for this dog."

The money was counted out, handed over, and a receipt taken.

"Now," said **Mr.** Hereford, "**you have sold** me this dog for five **hundred dollars**," and, as he said so, **he** again pressed the button, **at** which a door opened, and the police detective stood behind the man, as he answered, " I have sold him."

At the very instant the culprit felt a heavy hand on his shoulder, and heard the terrible words, " You are arrested for stealing this dog from the house of Mrs. Akmé this evening."

The detective then remarked to Mr. Hereford that this dog had been returned to Mrs. Akmé the day before by Mr. De Noo in person, but had now been, this evening, during the absence of the ladies, stolen a second time by the butler Harman, in the expectation of making a second sale.

This was a curious bit of news for Mr. Hereford, as to the practical working of his own advertisement, but he made no comment other than to say to the officer, " You have my sincere thanks for this zealous performance of your duty, and you deserve to be placed in charge of the detective service. Further than this, and regarding the refunding of the five hundred dollars, my secretary will confer with you."

So saying, he left the room, where stood the trembling rascal, who had been lured into his net, the secretary who was to attend to the matter as a business transaction, and the officer, who was now ready to march off with his prisoner.

In another instant a servant entered to say to the detective that Mr. Hereford would see that the dog was at once returned to Mrs. Akmé, and in fifteen minutes a cab drove off with the still slumbering creature in the arms of his butler, with a note from Mr. Hereford.

Mrs. Akmé had been so perplexed and bewildered by the endearing words that she had unwittingly heard Mr. Hereford address to Alma, that, had not her painful doubts been met by entire candor, some serious distrust must have ensued, such as that gentleman hoped might be the case.

There is just one thing that the man who succeeds by deceiving others never seems to take properly into his plots, and that is the atmosphere of lucid truth that protects the single-hearted.

Scarcely had Lennox Montague made his formal bow to her and departed, than Alma, with passionate weeping, repeated to Mrs. Akmé, word for word, the entire conversation with Mr. Hereford that evening. She told her all, every word, not even keeping back the stinging reproach, that cut so deeply, of Mrs. Akmé's supporting her as an object of charity. ' Had she been versed for a lifetime in the subtle arts of diplomacy she could not have done a wiser thing; for as the distressed girl made known her sorrow as rapidly as heart-breaking sobs permitted the utterance, the iniquity of the intention to take advantage of any technicality of the law to entrap to her destruction this lovely being became evident to Mrs. Akmé, whose wide experience of the world gave her a clear insight of character.

She was also somewhat prepared by her own observation that evening to find this man of momentous enterprises false, for she had been shocked by his cool declaration of having forgotten Ysolde Lennox, and his uncivil demeanor to

her son, as she had not forgotten the school-girl
confidences of Ysolde to her in his regard. And
rejected addresses are never quite overlooked
When Alma had, upon her first coming to her,
related the outlines of her previous history,
the letter of the cousin who had cast her off so
cruelly had been spoken of, but the name of
the writer had not been given, nor had Mrs.
Akmé cared to hear it. But in the light of
present revelations it assumed real importance.

While these two harassed women were still
in deep consultation over the difficulties to be
overcome, a violent pull at the door-bell, several times repeated, attracted their attention.

"It is after one o'clock," said Mrs. Akmé,
"and poor Harman naturally must have some
time for sleep. We cannot expect our people
to serve us night and day, for they really need
rest far more than we do. He is such a faithful man, so attentive and obliging, I will not
disturb him."

At this, the bell rang again, with a pull that
threatened breakage, and Alma said, "Let me

answer the bell," at the same instant hastening to open the door. Mrs. Akmé, thinking it somewhat of a risk at that time of night to open a front door, followed Alma so closely that she heard her immediate exclamation of surprise.

As the door was closed there stood Alma holding Chim in her arms, carefully wrapped in his eider-down quilt, and fast asleep.

Exclamation followed exclamation, and the surprise was so great that no heed had been given to the note that accompanied his return, although, of course, it must give the sought-for explanation.

How often do people hold in their hands a sealed letter or package to their address, examining the chirography and the superscription, and even wondering who it is from, when, perhaps, after a few moments of such dazed unconsciousness, they open and read, and are provoked at their own stupidity or absent-mindedness. There would seem to be so many occasions in our lives when we act as two distinct entities.

"Oh, Alma!" said Mrs. Akmé, "the note!"

"True," she answered, "how dull I am!" and she opened and read aloud the following:

My dearest kinswoman: **Mrs.** Akmé's butler, Harman, has been arrested for stealing **your** dog while you **and** she were both away this evening. I am happy to send Chim back to you unharmed. **He has** evidently been **drugged to keep** him **quiet,** but **doubtless** by **morning** will **be all right.** The revelations of **this evening, my** dearest cousin, have brought a hope of happiness to my desolated home. As your **legal guardian and only** surviving relative, it will be my pleasing **duty to trans-** fer you, in the course of the next **few days, from the** kind **and** considerate hospitality of your acquaintance, Mrs. Akmé, **and place you before the world where you ought to be, not only as the lovely** mistress presiding **over** my establishment, but also as **my** adopted daugh- **ter** and ward.

> **Ever your** devoted kinsman,
> BUNCOMBE HEREFORD.

Upon reading this, to them, terrible letter, Chim's rescue, her man's unfaithfulness, and all were forgotten, as, with a great fear of the near impending danger, these **women,** who tenderly loved each other, wept in each **other's arms.** But Mrs. Akmé was, if possible, more terrified

than was Alma, because she better understood
the depths of villainy, and saw more clearly
into the designing arts of this wicked man.

"How old are you, my darling?" she asked
Alma, who replied, "I am just twenty."   .

And Mrs. Akmé shuddered as she thought
that for one year the blessed child would be
legally under her guardian's care. And she,
who so lately had run the gamut of skepticism,
of agnosticism, of theosophy, and kindred fallacies, lifted her woman's heart to God, pray-
ing Him to protect in His own perfect way this
lamb of His flock. Little did she imagine how
near is the answer whenever prayer ascends,
piercing the earth-clouds that hide alike from
view His avenging and His shielding arm. But
Alma's ignorance of the real gravity of the perils
that surrounded her spared her some of this
misery, and the dawn found her tranquilly
sleeping, while Mrs. Akmé still walked the
floor, viewing and reviewing in her mind all
the aspects of the dangerous complications
they might so soon have to meet.

As the result of the long vigil, she determined to hold on to Alma as if she were her
own beloved daughter, and to employ, if need
be, the best legal talent, at no matter what
cost, in the contest; and if it was thought that
her guardian must have control of his ward
until the expiration of his term of guardian-
ship, she would, if it came to the worst, clan-
destinely leave the country during that time
with her precious treasure. And one of her
desperate resolves was—for one gets desperate
in the long, wakeful watches of a night—if it
would insure additional protection in case they
had to seek concealment, they would even
"farm out" Chim, on the plan of the well-taken-
care-of French babies.

And having finally marked out a course of
action she, too, fell asleep in the broad light of
morning, only to start and moan in troubled
dreams, full of hair-breadth escapes and a
never-ending kidnapping of both Alma and
Chim.

CHAPTER XI

THE morning succeeding the *musicale* Mrs.
Akmé sent a note to Lennox Montague, requesting him to call and see her on a matter
of business as soon as possible.

Now, after Lennox had escorted the ladies
home that evening when he had received the
shock of hearing those fateful words addressed
to Alma, he, too, had passed a sleepless night.

The soul never seems to know herself until
she is questioned. She stands, as it were, a
mute sentinel at the ever-open portal of the
senses, but speaks not with the clear, still voice
of the spirit, amid the torrential sweep and the
bubbling turmoil that go to make up the busy
excitement of the broad and rapid flow of life's
onward progress. But presently the hitherto

unheeded force of passionate impulse, the accumulating exterior pressure, drifts us upon some hidden rock, or unheeded quicksands, and then we cry out to the pilot at the helm.

So Lennox had not realized, or, realizing, had failed to measure, how deeply his happiness was involved by his love for Alma, until the sharp blow, thus rudely given, had forced upon him its terrible realization. But now, as he reviewed again and again all that had transpired between them, although he had claimed no avowal of interest from her, yet had there not been that satisfying interchange of thought, those sympathetic glances giving unspoken words that no language could so well express, that had made him feel, without the asking, that she was indeed the *alter ego* of the best that was in him, the *eidolon* of his dreams, the chiefest, the one supreme blessing, the idealization of happiness for him ?

Could she thus have met him, and at the same time held in her heart a superior affection for another, and that other a man too old to share the fresh emotions of a young girl's tender fancy?

Then, had he not understood that virtually they were strangers to each other?

Was it possible that this pure and high-minded girl could have been so readily influenced or at all controlled by the great wealth and power of this man arising from such an ascendancy?

But this suspicion was at once set aside as an unworthy thought regarding such a woman.

And yet how could he ever forget having heard those endearing words applied to her by one whose age and position would alike prevent any mistake on his part?

There must have been some strong reason to have prompted and permitted such sudden advances.

It was one of those inexplicable occurrences that became more and more mysterious as one tried to fathom it, or even penetrate into its motives.

Oppressed by this ever-increasing gloom

and uncertainty, he was at a loss what course to take, and he was depressed by conflicting agitations when he received Mrs. Akmé's note. It brought some ray of hope, as he asked himself if it were not connected with the painful subject of his meditations. "Ah," he said, "perhaps kind Heaven vouchsafes at least a clue to guide me in this outer darkness in which I grope bewildered."

So he hastened to seek Mrs. Akmé.

The revelations that she had to make, as she told him all that had taken place, distressing as it was to hear that Alma was subjected to such shameful persecution, yet, compared to his fears, brought a relief so great that he was positively happy.

His admiration of the brave girl was unbounded as he heard the whole recital, for he never before had fully known the sharp trials to which she had been subjected during all these past years of her clouded youth.

When Mrs. Akmé had concluded her story, she added: "Lennox, perhaps you are too young to give safe advice in a matter of such moment, but you have a good legal mind, some knowledge of law, a warm heart, and you are staunch and true, so I wish to know exactly what you think."

He did not reply for a few minutes, and it was evident that he was much agitated.

Then he said : " The peril is doubtless great, but it does not seem to me to be as grave as you apprehend, my dear Mrs. Akmé. Miss Aylwyn has reached an age when, certainly, any court would permit her to decide as to her domicile. I fancy that the extraordinary course Mr. Hereford proposes to take must be rather in the expectation of imposing upon her presumed want of knowledge of her legal rights, rather than from any fixed intention of really forcing her will."

" Then you do not think that Alma could be constrained to leave me against her consent ?"

" At her age I do not," said Lennox. " The real danger, rather, consists in the powerful,

almost irresistible, weight that such a man as
Hereford can bring to bear to crush those who
incur his displeasure. Where a man controls
such vast interests, there are existing ramifica-
tions affecting so many others that it is difficult to say what harm may ensue."

"I see," said Mrs. Akmé; "and it is not easy
to know how to avert an unforeseen peril."

"There is always this comfort," said Lennox,
"that law does protect the helpless, and if,
through its various intricacies, it may at times
fail in so doing, it is not on account of its inef-
ficiency, but rather owing to the ignorance of
those who appeal to its protection. I hold it
as almost absolutely certain that under the
handling of a well-trained and learned lawyer
one cannot be injured without obtaining ample
redress."

"Dear Lennox," interrupted Mrs. Akmé,
"you inspire me with confidence. You have,
I see, an old head on young shoulders."

"I trust not," said he, smiling, "for I would
rather be altogether young, and, may I add,

so pleasing as to be acceptable to Miss Aylwyn."

"What do you mean?" asked Mrs. Akmé, with a sudden start.

"I mean, my dear friend," he answered gravely, "that I love this charming woman with my whole heart and soul and far more than my own life."

"You would not," said Mrs. Akmé turning pale, "seek to take her from me? It is an unexpected possibility that you suggest."

"Your fears are premature in my regard," answered he with a sad smile, "for as yet I have not ventured to tell her of my love, nor have I any assurance that Miss Aylwyn cares for me."

Mrs. Akmé instantly recalled various expressions of Alma, or, rather, little incidents, before unnoted, that now seemed to take shape. "I fancy," she said, "that you might engage her interest."

"Pardon any seeming indiscretion on my part," said he, "but I have the courage to mention this subject of deepest import to me because, if Miss Aylwyn would but accept my protection, the law would consider the claim of a husband as paramount to that of any guardian."

"Ah! I see," said Mrs. Akmé. "Such a happy contingency would put an end to any danger from this dreaded interference. Oh, Lennox, only promise to make your home with me, and you may go with my blessing and make known your love to this dear girl."

At this moment a strain of melody from Alma's harp reached them.

Lennox arose. "With your permission, my dear madam," he said, "I will join her; but how can I hope to secure so much happiness? It is presumption."

A moment later Lennox paused at the open door of the music-room involuntarily, in admiration.

Alma stood at her harp, and heaped in confusion at her feet were the various pieces of music she had tried and in her concentered mood thrown aside for still others that replaced them, until, having, as it were, wearied with these harmonies, her spirit had awakened to its own musical concepts.

Thus with one arm resting lovingly on the instrument, the other hand with caressful touches framed snatches of thought into plaintive, soul-stirring, spiritualized utterance.

Lennox, entranced, caught the *motif*, and followed with musical enthusiasm the sweet succession of improvised sound, with its changing intermixture of warmth, color, light, shadow, interwoven with depth, fervor, and *nuances* of delicious delicacy, the outpouring of creative inspiration; and in his rapture he forgot that Alma was unaware of his presence, but, catching the refrain, sang in unison with her theme.

What glimpses of heaven on earth does not music bring, wafting to our ardent longings echoes of the eternal hymns!

Alma turned with glad surprise as Lennox joined her, and she gave the accompaniment

of an air, which Lennox sang with much taste
and feeling.

Then she stopped and, extending her hand,
said frankly: "I am ever so happy to see you,
Mr. Montague; I was trying to forget my
sorrow;" and, as if she could not control the
sudden sense of desolation, she clasped her
hands in an attitude of deep dejection.

"Alma," said Lennox—"permit me to say
Alma—Mrs. Akmé has just told me all. Do
not, I beg you, be dismayed at the intrigues
of this unscrupulous schemer. May I dare to
tell you, at such a time, that your love means
life for me? Give me, dear Alma," he continued with impassioned earnestness and taking
her hand, "the right to protect you as your
husband."

Alma was silent.

"Ah, do not, do not," he begged, "refuse to
become my wife."

And Alma said: "Lennox, I love you; it
were needless to deny it, but I cannot be your
wife."

"My darling," he exclaimed, "may Heaven forever bless you for the assurance of your love! But why, then, may I not hope that you will be mine?"

"Because I love you too truly," she said.

"I cannot understand, dear Alma," he replied.

"Listen, Lennox," she answered. "I am but a poor orphan girl. My cousin tells me I am an object of charity. You are but starting out in your business career, having yet your fortune to make, and I cannot at the very outset of your honorable efforts allow you to take upon yourself the added weight of my support."

"Fear not for our united future, my beloved Alma," he said, "for happiness, love and content compel success. You will be my chiefest aid, and through you my star will be in the ascendant. But if, on the contrary, you refuse me this needed succor, from whatever motive, you will then, indeed, mar my whole career."

"Dear Lennox," she said, "let us first have the patience of seemly waiting for a time. We have in reality scarcely known each other, although, it must be confessed, we have always been in sympathy. Since my cousin has reminded me, I must not forget that he educated me for a teacher; and, thinking it over, I shall better endure a dependence dear, generous Mrs. Akmé forbids me to think of, but which, none the less, exists, if she will be so good as to let me give music-lessons."

"But, dear Alma," expostulated Lennox, "Mrs. Akmé asks you to take the place of her own daughter. She would never permit you to do this."

"I think, Lennox, that she would when she understands that it is necessary for my own self-respect," she replied.

Mrs. Akmé was so anxious that she could no longer stay away, so she entered at this moment, and said to them in a loving way:

"I am sure, my children, that you love each other, and I trust that you have found out that you do."

And Lennox answered: "Dear mother, as

your adopted children we crave your blessing."

Then she blessed them as her very own.

"I have told Lennox that we must wait in
all patience, for as yet we cannot marry," said
Alma.

"Not so, dear," said Mrs. Akmé; "you need
the immediate protection that Lennox can give
you.   Then his right will be superior to that of
your guardian."

At this, Alma, who could always be reasoned
with, being superior in this respect to the gen-
erality of mankind, looked very serious, and
the whole matter was carefully reviewed in all
its aspects, the conclusion being that if Mr.
Hereford endangered her stay with Mrs. Akmé
by his persistency, she would then marry Lennox at once.   But otherwise the engagement
would not be announced, but affairs would remain in abeyance.

"Ah," sighed Alma, "could I but only regain the dear old homestead, which, it does
seem, should have remained by right as ours,

then I would not feel so—in spite of all your tender love—so like an object of charity," and she burst into tears.

Then Mrs. Akmé, kissing her, said, "I never, never can forgive that brutal man for his cruel speech."

It is strange how all the leading events of life are accompanied by lesser incidents, as if there were always, in the ebb and flow of the tide of human action, wavelets of reflex motion. So it was in this instance, for as Lennox and Alma attained this climacteric period leading up to their united existence—a sort of high-tide movement, as it were—Chim, who had played such an important part as the immediate cause of their knowing each other at all, was an un-observed, but not an unobservant, spectator of all that had just taken place. But he had that wis-dom, notwithstanding his deep interest in what was going on, that comparatively few mortals possess, of keeping absolute silence at the prop-er time; nor did he by any movement obtrude his presence even when Mrs. Akmé entered.

And now comes the astounding proof that a wise dog does know his own master, even when that master is a new one, for when Lennox went away, Chim, without making the least sign of what he was going to do, slyly followed him in silence. Of course Chim knew perfectly, having seen, heard, and watched the entire proceedings, that Alma was too agitated—in fact, each of the *dramatis personæ* had been too occupied—to notice him, and yet he felt it due to the occasion to act his own part properly and make a respectful act of allegiance to Lennox. He therefore meekly followed this man of Alma's choice to his office, and so preoccupied was Lennox that it was not until he had seated himself at his desk that Chim thought the time had come to attract his attention.

Lennox knew all about dogs, and so at once understood that Chim wished to say to him that he adopted Lennox as one of the family. So, taking Chim in his arms, he stroked, petted, caressed and praised him for the delicate compliment in his regard. At the same time

he explained to Chim that it was the wish of
Alma that the engagement should not be
known, and that he must, therefore, not follow
him around. Whereupon, taking a cab, he at
once returned Chim to his mistress, who must
have somewhat mortified the dog's vanity by
saying that she had not been aware of his
absence.

Ah, Chim! although you bore a part in this
life-drama, yet in this one act you were not
missed.

"I hurried back with him, dear Alma," said
Lennox, laughing, "for fear that he might, by
his devoted attentions, make the announcement
before you were ready to permit it."

"The very thoughtful act of a true cavalier,"
said Alma. "Thanks."

That very day that Alma and Lennox were
affianced the air seemed propitious for lovers,
for about the same hour that the little love-
scene just narrated was enacted at Mrs. Akmé's,
Mr. Marquis La Fayette de Noo, finding the
pretty Annette in the upper hall alcove alone,

sat down on a *tabouret* beside her to assist her
by handing out of a basket near by the *nœuds*
of rose-colored ribbons with which a ball-dress
of Miss Marie Jeanne was being trimmed.

"Annette," he asked, "how is it that you
happen to understand my English so well?"

She laughed a little laugh that sounded like
the low tinkling of a silver bell, and answered:

"Of course, *your* English is not easy to understand, yet why should I not speak the language and understand it too?"

"Because," answered Marquis, "I never
heard of any Frenchwoman talking as you do."

"I will tell you a little secret," she said mysteriously, "if you will promise to keep it to
yourself."

"'Pon honor I promise," he answered, "for
I am just dying to hear."

"With curiosity such as women have?" she
asked.

"I confess to far more," said he; "I've just
one minute to bear this suspense and live."

"Well, then," she said, "it's a dead **secret,** but I'm not a Frenchwoman at all."

"Maybe, then," said he, "you're a Russian **Nihilist, an** Italian countess, a German **frau-**lein, or an English governess?"

"**You** shall never know," she answered poutingly.

"You needn't confess," **cried he,** "for **I** know for sure **and** certain that **you're the** loveliest little witch since the Creation, when one came out of the Garden of Eden."

"**You've** guessed just right," said she; "I've changed my mind again, and if you will keep **quiet, and** not rumple those silk bows, **I'll** tell **you a** little history just as it came **to** pass: **Well,** once upon a time there lived a young girl in the Wooden Nutmeg State, **and** she was a moth-erless lass. She had a big brother—please take a note of that—but no sister, and her father was a farmer, who had at one time been a miner and **'made his pile,'** and speculated and **lost it all, ex-**cept enough to buy a farm of stones, **briars and** thistles **with.** So this girl, who looked as I do,

and whose name was Anne Larens, had to go to
a hotel in Northampton in summer as a wait-
ress so as to get enough money for her winter's
schooling.   And there were other farmers'
daughters who did the same thing, and it was
thought no disgrace for us.   But one day there
arrived at the hotel a very rich invalid old
lady, who took a great fancy to Anne and
would have the girl travel with her; and so,
when the father found that the heart of his
daughter was set on it he let her go, just for a
little, to see the world.   Then she went over to
Europe, where, after traveling about for some
time, the old lady suddenly died in Paris.
Now, just at that sad time, when Anne was
unexpectedly left alone in a foreign country,
and had to get back to America the best way
she could, a very rich American lady advertised for a French maid."

"And you offered yourself, Annette," Mark
interrupted.

"In the first place," replied the girl, blushing, "my name is not Annette, but Anne

Larens, and, in the second place, I'm heartily ashamed to confess that necessity compelled me to represent myself as French. But I have been faithful, and tried to do more than a French maid would consent to do."

"Ha, ha!" laughed Mark; "it's the drollest thing I ever heard."

"As to my French," said Anne, "it has passed muster and been better understood for the liberal use of English; but, candidly, I've been very unhappy on account of the deceit, and I have written to father that I'm here, and will come to him so soon as my place can be filled."

"No you won't, dear Anne," exclaimed Mark, respectfully taking her hand and kissing it, "for I can't live without you. I would rather work on your father's farm with your big brother, than dawdle away my time here when you go."

"You are not spoiled, but manly, after all," replied Anne; "but I've more pride, perhaps, than you think for, Mark, and for all the world

I wouldn't run away with you and have it said I had entrapped you by my arts."

" If you loved me," said he ruefully, " you would be willing to marry me and take my name."

" A name of Mark," she slyly suggested.

" But here comes the governor," said he; " I hear the fog-horn "—by which euphony his son referred to a way his father had of using a huge red silk bandana.

" Do, dear Anne, say yes or no to a man— do you love me ? *Don't* say no."

" Yes," whispered she, and he just had time to snatch a kiss in grateful recognition and declare that he wasn't good enough by half, when they were interrupted.

" Father," said he, taking Anne's hand, " I love this young woman, and have told her so, but she will never marry me unless you say yes. Give us your blessing, I beg you."

There was a dew drop in Larry Noo's eye as he looked at the handsome young couple who stood before him. He gazed at them

some minutes, then sadly shook his head, saying :

"I'm sorry, my boy; I don't mind her being
poor, for I was once a poor boy myself, and
I've worked up. She's a likely young woman,
too. Well, I'm awful sorry, but the long and
the short of it is, Mark, I can't go the French."

Mark, who at first had looked very lugubri-
ous, at this unexpected ending actually shouted, ·
he laughed so; he cut a double pigeon-wing,
then shook hands with the old gentleman, crying out : "All right, governor! we're yours
every time—she's a Yankee girl. *Hurrah !*"

"You don't say so!" exclaimed Larry Noo
opening his eyes wide; "I thought there was
good in her. But say, Mark, how did she catch
that infernal jingo so pat ? "

So the three sat down on the sofa, the governor between them, and the lover told the
whole story, with very complimentary flour-
ishes in behalf of Anne, but when he came
to the name—Anne Larens—his father cried
out :

"Bless me! what was your father's name, Anne?"

"When he was a miner, sir, he was called 'Towhead Bill,' because of his light hair," she answered.

Whereupon, Larry Noo just opened wide his brawny, honest, helpful arms, and giving the pretty maid a tight squeeze, exclaimed: "Well, I declare, it's too good to be true—Bill Larens's daughter! Why, girl, I just loved your father; but promise me, Anne, there'll be none of that *polly-voos*. I just hate it; it takes all the starch out of a man."

"Never a word, sir; we both hate it," laughed Anne.

"The Lord be praised for all his mercies!" said Larry Noo devoutly. "Now, children, do as I say: Don't waste time; take a cab; take a wedding trip; go to Philadelphia; telegraph me from there when you're married."

"And mother and Sis?" asked Mark.

"It'll be pretty tough for me at first," said Larry Noo wincing; "but leave that to me, children, for," he added, with great feeling, "it'll be the making of you, my boy; and here's the needful to start with."

So saying, he pulled a fat pocket-book out, handing it to his son.

"Oh, sir," said Anne, "you are indeed one of nature's noblemen."

"Not a word of that, Anne," said he. "I'm plain Larry Noo."

"Pardon me, sir," said she; "I love Mark, but if I marry him he must work, and make a man of himself."

"I'd expect as much," said Larry Noo admiringly, "from Billy Larens's daughter— that's the true ring in it, Anne."

"If you say so, father, this dear plucky little woman and I will try it in Dakota, where a man may work up to something."

"I'd like to go there myself," said Larry Noo enthusiastically. "It's a blessed place for freedom, where every man can smoke, speak and spit as he pleases. But go now," he added nervously. "I'll express the trunks after you—go, before mother and Sis come home."

And just as these ladies drove up to the door a cab was turning the corner, in which were two happy, happy lovers on their way to Philadelphia and matrimony.

CHAPTER XII

CHIM SUB ROSA

IN the feverish excitement incident to rapid money-making in this country, it will now and then occur that combinations and trusts, similar to the one of which Buncombe Hereford was president, will inveigle the unwary. They should rather be called mistrusts.

Even as some overshadowing tree, that absorbs, as it grows, endless solar rays which are hidden in its opaque substance, collecting a thousand, thousand influences toward its vast increase, holding its varied elements in close cohesion, and only reproducing its hitherto impervious light through combustion, and, with the glare of desolating conflagration, leaving naught but a residuum of ashes, so Buncombe Hereford, as the master-spirit of this trust, knew that the first incandescent sparks had already laid the train for that fierce burning. He foresaw that the hollow shams of watered stocks, fraudulent issues, flattering promises, brilliant circulars, hypothecated mineral lands, as securities that had no real existence, and paper towns of alluring aspect, must collapse —he knew that this network of fraud could not be indefinitely floated.

He had expected, by a sort of hocus-pocus familiar to those experts who handle big schemes, to be able to inflate the market, sell his bonds at high figures, and stand from under with bloated wealth when the inevitable crash must come. But his distended balloon had become unwieldy and soared out of reach.

Under the terrible pressure of the swift-coming doom, insomnia, that grim scourge of the overcrowded brain and of spent force, took possession of him and exhausted his remaining nerve power.

Already some days had elapsed since he sent that note to Alma which gave her so much uneasiness, but the multiplied and harassing cares that beset him had caused a delay in the execution of a set purpose, whose fruition, after all, was but a mere passing pleasure, the plucking of a wayside flower that bloomed in his path. Like other whims of fancy, it could be allowed momentarily to rest, while events would assist in development when he was prepared to act.

A day of great and harassing disappointments had just closed, whose culminating point had been the summons to appear before a certain congressional committee for an investigation that he was in no wise prepared to meet.

Being thus unexpectedly hunted down and brought to bay, he concluded to try an evasive policy—quietly leave town and retire to the old Virginia homestead until the time would come to double on his track and reappear. It would be understood that he had been suddenly called to London to confer with some leading capitalists. Meantime, in order to solace some coming idle hours, he would take his pretty ward with him, and introduce her to

the old homestead, which really was hers. He
felt that he was but an usurper under its shel-
tering roof.

The business complications that he had
represented to Alma's mother as existing had
as their sole cause his own fraudulent use of
their means, in exchange for which he had doled
out a stinted allowance during the lifetime of
Alma's mother, and, after her death, had her
daughter educated in order to support herself.
Nor was he in any strict legal sense, as he assumed to be, Alma's guardian, or she his ward.
But Buncombe Hereford knew the weight of
assumptions and plausible assertions, for from
beginning to end his career could have been
summed up in five letters—*fraud*. One thing
had been commented upon very quietly in that
part of the country where the old manor-house
was—that no will had ever been found of Alma's
Grandfather Hereford. He was a prudent old
gentleman, and it was thought curious, to say
the least, that a man of large estate should
have died intestate. But in that matter his

nephew was actually innocent, for he, as well as others, knew nothing of any testamentary papers. Hereford had made strict but vain search at the old place when he was there.

He expected to have a busy day on the morrow, for the day after he would go down to the old Virginia homestead, taking Alma with him.

Sleep was sadly needed. He had walked the floor for several hours; all his immediate plans were matured, and what was now the paramount necessity was some hours of rest. But he was never wider awake. There was a dull ache in the back of the neck, as if his head was supported with difficulty; now and then shooting pains passed through the temples, which work and worry and wakefulness might readily cause.

"It is the neuralgic air of Washington," thought he; "I will compel sleep."

He knew that to seek the bed would but keep him wide awake, so, reclining in a luxurious *chaise-longue* in a half recumbent posture, he muttered: "I know it can be done—I will hypnotize myself, and my weary mind shall demand and **gain the** mastery **over its** slave, **the body."**

A red-shaded lamp placed in a **corner** of the room threw a small circle of roseate light upon the ceiling, and this point he selected for experiment. So, fixing his gaze intently with the full force of his will power on the radius of the quivering diameter, he presently fell under his own hypnotic power.

And now a strange and weird sensation took possession **of him.** He had grasped the thunderbolt and played with **the** electric lightning's **thrill, but it brought with** it elemental dissolution; almost at once he began to have the horrible realization that he was slowly, **but surely,** separating from his dual self.

He tried in vain to resist this painful division, for he dearly loved, nay, worshiped, his own indivisible *Ego,* **and** he must have and retain every particle **of himself.** But his gaze was firmly riveted upon this small **luminous circumference, and** he was unable to divert it.

It was rapidly increasing in its intensity, and had now become a crystal filled with odylic power, and speeding forth innumerous rays that shot through the full tension of his brain with millions, billions, trillions of infinitesimal magnetic points, that caused the most horrible pricking, burning, flashing pains. Yet the sheer agony of it all was, that out of the depths of this burning crystal, as in a flaming focus, there came forth, one by one, in endless procession, the compulsory review of the sins of a lifetime.

Nothing could be palliated or hidden when made clear by that radiant magic mirror, upon whose telltale surface, before the assembled throngs of curious, jibing onlookers that now appeared in dim outline above, below, around him, filling up all space, and smothering him down by the vast concourse that ever grew. Ah, yes; these were the accusing souls—some writhen, distorted features he began to recognize, and they, one and all, in silence pointed to the merciless, transparent surface of that crystal

No voice spake, but he was made to understand: " These are your accusers, and the burning crystal is *truth*, before which stands your naked soul, stripped of all disguises."

He groaned, and foamed; and raged under the torture, but never one cry for mercy escaped that proud spirit. No penitential tear was shed to wipe out with its purifying brightness the dark stains ; not one prayer of true contrition ascended to redeem the soul that hung suspended in the balance, and the pitying ange turned away, its translucent wings, poised heavenward to save, now folded, sad-drooping.

And then, amidst the ravings of his despair, last and chiefest appeared the mouthing, jibbering face of his once beautiful wife, whose senseless, lunatic expression dominated every other image; and, as if in shadow, also rose to view the reproachful eyes of Alma. No forms appeared, for he only saw the agonized face of his wife and the penetrating gaze of Alma.

And during this mental torment was the physical one of being rent apart.

Now he is dual. He grasps at an ethereal subtle vapor that vainly seeks to repossess the senses, but it is thrust aside by a grosser fluidic substance, that forms into terrible shape, that with menace takes possession, and, with the infinite yearning that the lost soul alone can know, there fades away out of his brutal grasp that outraged purer principle that had made its life-struggle in vain. Oh, most horrible fate! to have, with one's own volition, cast forth the spiritual essence!

Disembodied from this higher life he began to sink, clogged heavily by the weight of the dull form that bore him downward—he was dying, and loosened was his clinging hold of Earth.

The thread of life could no longer endure the tension of that irresistible momentum. Then he fell heavily, the strong will, that had made him adhere so tenaciously to himself, snapped asunder like a broken reed, and, having heaped full and running over the measure of his misdeeds, Buncombe Hereford was dead. He was dead—*or*, being hypnotized, he was mistaken for dead, and buried as dead.

.   .   .   .

The *abracadabra* of society, that which renovates its feeble vitality and preserves it from entire inanition, is *gossip*, that, like the inverted cone of this ancient mystic triangle which begins with next to nothing, spreading out by repetition to such broad dimensions that it is surprising how it remains self-sustaining, and yet it simply begins with the first person, who says "A," the next adds, and says "A B," and so on, and so forth.

But the day succeeding the sensational elopement of Marquis La Fayette de Noo, and the tragic suddenness of the taking off of the Trust Magnate, was indeed a regular red-letter day, a windfall mercifully given, too, just as the gay season had closed, and the insufferable dullness of Lent had set in.

These two events, under their relatively comical and serious aspects, formed what is called "the staple of conversation" during no end of

luncheons and the *petit-soupers* that characterize Lenten devotions at the capital.

The saints of the deserts fasted and prayed,
but we have changed all that in this nineteenth
century, for now it is said, "they feasted and
prayed." Why not? asks Society.

It would take a library of such books as "A
Washington Season," and "A Washington
Winter," to narrate the half that was volubly
repeated on this occasion. Even Chim, who
had had his card engraved "Mr. Chim," made
visits, and been *par excellence* the social
lion, although as yet he had not scratched up
ten thousand a month—even Chim was no
longer in apogee!

Yet, could these agitated social circles have
heard with their own polite ears, or seen with
their own critical eyes, what really took place
when the ladies De Noo returned from that
drive, it would have been more satisfying.

As it was, the French valet who stood in the
adjoining room that day saw all, but understood imperfectly. His imagination, however,

supplied the missing links when he communicated his impressions, with appropriate gestures, to the French maid of Mrs. MacKane, and she told the English footman of Mr. Tom Noodles, who told his master, and that accomplished *raconteur* lost no time in giving a club dinner, for there was something more rare than terrapin stew or canvas-back to serve up—there was the recital of a *bona-fide* scene.

But Larry Noo himself is the best authority, and there is extant the longest letter he ever wrote, for business correspondence is always limited-express matter. This racy epistle, addressed to his son Mark, gives the long and the short of what happened on the return home of the ladies De Noo on that fateful morning.

The moment they entered, Mrs. La Fayette de Noo directed a servant to "send for Annette" to take off her wraps, as she was too tired out even to ascend in the lift before lunching.

The smiling footman, butler, second man, and parlor maid all joined in a still hunt, which of course proved unavailing.

Mrs. La Fayette de Noo remembered that animating incident of the old French monarch, who would rather die than be assisted by the wrong functionary, and she proposed to be in good form.

The maid was wanted to remove madame's hat, wrap and gloves, and the maid alone would madame have.

Meantime Marie Jeanne, who was less permeated with the heroism of *noblesse oblige*, ran up-stairs to her room, but soon came bouncing down, quite like an excited schoolgirl.

"Mère," she cried, "Annette's gone! I don't as yet miss anything, but of course something's gone with her."

"I'm in a way," cried Mrs. La Fayette de Noo, much flustered. "Nobody here to take off my *gants*."

"If you're upset, mère," suggested the young lady, who was ever ready to take his remedies, "send for Dr. Mensana."

"No, I won't," replied the mère, with considerable vivacity; "he'll advise a muster-plaster."

"What's the matter, ladies?" tenderly inquired Mr. Lafayette de Noo, who at this moment made his appearance, and whose prolonged residence in Washington was making him diplomatic.

"Annette! Annette!" they both bawled out in chorus.

"Let me take her place, since she's otherwise engaged," suggested he with a bow.

"I declare," thought his wife, "he's next to equal of the French minister, Larry is."

Perceiving the bland look of his spouse, he stooped over, untied her bonnet-strings, loosened her head-gear, and actually imprinted a kiss right in the middle of her forehead, for he felt some sorrow and more compunction in her regard.

"Oo! Oo!" she cried, quickly clapping her gloved hands to the frizzes that were pinned on to the top of her cranium, but which, having been dislodged by Larry's unpinning, now tumbled off in a mass. "Oo, Oo! *me che-vaux !*"

"Gemini, mother !" cried the unfortunate, stepping back amazed and aghast at the devastation. "Have I scalped you? I feel like a real, live, wild Injun."

"Worse an' worser nor that !" she cried. "I'm in dishabille. Where's Mark ?"

": True enough," remarked Marie Jeanne. "You bet *he* knows where Annette is."

"He does," replied Larry, with a big Adam's apple sticking in his throat. "I saw them drive off together !"

"*You* saw them, and didn't stop them!" cried his wife in astonishment. "Just them two *en-famille ?*"

"The French part of it warn't there," said *pater-familias.*

"Well, it's come to a pretty pass," cried Miss Marie Jeanne, tossing her head, "when a hoity-toity maid takes a ride with a De Noo ! When she comes back, I'll just ship her over the sea to France."

"But she won't come back," said her father gravely.

"And what am I to do *sans* a French maid?" asked his wife.

"Take me, or take an Irish one, mother," suggested he.

"Mr. La Fayette de Noo," expostulated she with dignity, "this, sir, is adding insult to injury. I wish my son Marquis was here."

"He won't come back either," said he doggedly.

"Where's Mark gone to?" both exclaimed.

"To be married to Anne Larens, thanks be to a merciful Providence," said his father defiantly.

The mother's face was a study at that moment, for, mixed with worry and rage, was a queer fancy that struck her. "I'm sure," she thought, "Annette was a French nobility in disguise. Mark's smart. He ought to be, he's my son, and he's just got her in time. I'll forgive them."

But Marie Jeanne cried out, "I'm going off

in a dead faint. Send for Dr. Mensana—quick."

But her father said, "No, you ain't, Mary Jane; your color's good and your voice strong. Smell camphor."

And the mother turning to him said very pleasantly, "Not Anne Larens, dear; you mean Annette."

Tender-hearted Larry Noo was quite overcome by the unexpected "dear," so taking her hand with a certain rude grace, he kissed it.

"He's getting just like a French Count," thought she, and she graciously repeated, "Annette, dear, and probably Annette de Montmorency. That's a real swell family in France."

This impeachment against Bill Larens's daughter was too much for Larry. So folding his arms and standing very straight and resolute, he said emphatically: "Let me tell you once for all, mother, she's a fine young woman and no French blood in her veins. She's a regular Yankee, and, I'm proud to say, old

Bill Larens's daughter, and no honester man than that same towhead Bill ever drew the breath of life."

"The deceitful wretch!" cried Marie Jeanne. "Send at once for Dr. Mensana. I'm very sick."

"And I'm worse'n sick," exclaimed the mother, rising majestically, "for I'm mad as a hornet."

"Now, mother," interrupted her husband, soothingly, "brace up."

"No, I won't!" she cried. "To have my hopes all dashed, just as I was looking forward to Mark's keeping up the family's dignity, to be based on them foreign nobility. If the girl had been a French maid, I could have bought her a pedigree of the French republic. But now she's old Bill Larens's girl, I'm heart-broke."

"But mother," interrupted her husband, condescending to make a favorable pointer, "she was smart about her French, wasn't she?"

"Yes," said she reflectively. "Annette was

cute enough, and I always understood her, so
of course, she spoke French as she is spoke."

"Shall I send for her to come back with
Mark?" asked he wistfully.

"No!" they both shrieked in chorus.

"The sooner you know it the better, Larry
Noo," said his wife. "What with your invin-
cible ignorance and Mark's goings on and off,
I give it up for a disgraced family. I won't
stay here no longer, nuther, for it's no place
to live in, no how, for people what has a pedigree and a crest. Then the actual, dense ignorance! So many citizens that speak English out and out. Not ten of them senators,
even, talk the pure Parisian, and they say
there's a kitchen cabinet—that's not French,
nuther."

"Why, mother," expostulated Larry, "of
course not. This is an American country."

"Call it by what name you please" said she.
"It's a new place. Why, just look at the old
Washingtonians, as they call themselves—they
don't look old at all. I'll go back and locate

in that gay Paris and ride every day to the Boys-de-Boolone, where even the babies lie round under the trees and call for 'lay' when they wants their bottles. The French goes so natural-like with them pert little dears."

"And I," said Marie Jeanne, "am bowed down with the disgrace—both me and Dr. Mensana."

"What's he got to do with this family? I guess we can manage ourselves," said her father angrily.

"He's to be one of us," said Marie Jeanne. "He's coming, as they do in France, in a day or two, to ask you and mère, and settle for the *dot*, and then he's going to marry me."

"The dot be d——d!" cried out her enraged parent. "He's an impudent fellow. I've heard of that sort of thing before. But he can't come that dodge over Larry Noo. Ain't a man satisfied to marry my daughter, but he must, like a highway robber, be asking for my purse, too?"

"But, père," interceded Marie Jeanne, coaxingly, taking his hand, "you wouldn't be so cruel as to cut off your loving, only daughter?"

Now Larry Noo had a big heart, and if you rubbed him or even stroked him but just a little the right way, he was as gentle as a great purring cat.

"Do you love this doctor, Sis?" he asked in a shaky voice.

"I wish to marry him," she answered. "He's made famous inventions. We wish to travel all over, and go to India and across the mountains there to Thibet, where he has some Silent Brothers, he says, and he will take things and instruments with him of his own proper invention, and he knows how to make more of the same kind out of a thing he has—a 'higher calculus' he calls it—and he has field glasses made on purpose to hunt up microbes and a bacilli and grippe insects and —"

"That's enough, Sis," said her father. "I see he's likely to be a handy man to have about the house, but you'll need a long purse to do all that, and travel all over the world, and feed all that circus. I'll settle on you, Sis, twenty-five thousand **dollars a** year, but not **a** red cent on him; and, my girl, he'll treat you all the kinder if you hold **him** with a short tether."

"What's **his** family?" asked the mother. "**Was his father** French?"

"No, mère," replied she. "He says his fa-·ther ought **to** have been French, he knows. But he's next best thing; his parents were a Mafia, and came **over from Italy** by way of France."

"If he can swear, Sis," said her good father, relenting, "that he's not one drop of the pol-ly-voos **in** him, and never expects to have, I'll **settle a** dot, which I suppose is French for pot **of gold, on him,** although I hate that same word. I'll let **it be** ten thousand **a year,** with **a proviso as long as he** treats you kind. And I wish him **good luck,** with his grasshoppers in the bargain, though he'll **never** catch as big a one as you are, again."

"But I don't like his having Silent Brothers,"

objected the mother, " for we might get mutes
in this family."

" Leave that mute business to me, mère,"
said Marie Jeanne as she disdainfully took her
departure to her room, without one word of
thanks, for she thought her father had been
very mean to her.

After she left, the mother asked, half crying,
"And who's to provide for me?"

"Your American husband, mother," said
Larry with a trembling voice. "If you *will*
go to Paris, I will go to Dakota with Mark and
Anne and Bill Larens. But you can do as
you please, mother, and depend on fifty thousand dollars a year to do it with. When I was
plain Larry Noo, and Bill and the rest of the
miners boarded in our shanty, you were a good,
faithful wife to me, and took care of us all.
You helped me at the start, fair and square,
mother, to make my pile, and you've earned
the right to your share. But we made one big
mistake, mother, when we separated for a time,
because I got that head over heels in work I

couldn't stop to breathe, and you women folks
wanted to travel and I let you stay too long.
You've come home, mother, with a French bee
in your bonnet, and mabbe it'll buzz some
more yet. But some day you'll be sick or
something, and want your Larry, and then—"

"Oh, Larry," she said, "I want you now.
Do come with me and be that Frenchman, or
buy up a title and be a Dook."

"Not if I know myself!" he cried energeti-
cally, "never! I'll go with Mark, for Washington's not overmuch to my taste anyhow.
There's too many foreigners here for me,
tacked onto jaw-splitting titles, and I'm plain
Larry Noo."

CHAPTER XIII

CHIM THE DISCOVERER

IT is to be hoped that the circumstance of its requiring thirteen chapters to chronicle the career of Chim may not prove an unlucky omen as regards the fate of this interesting creature.

An appeal is hereby made in his behalf to an indulgent public, to aid the writer in this attempt to prove the futility of a prejudice against the number thirteen, by giving Chim an encouraging reception, calculated to prolong his existence. Should he unhappily be strangled by falling under the weight of their displeasure within the year, his lamentable fate will then serve firmly to rivet this superstition in the popular mind.

The sudden death of Buncombe Hereford was very disastrous to the schemes of the speculators whom he represented, and not only caused an immediate collapse of the so-called "Trust," but also dragged down in the general ruin many well-deserving people, whose only fault had been either an unguarded credulity, or a fatal desire to grow suddenly rich. This untimely haste, this fever of greed, has caused many sober-minded people, who have the sense of discrimination and who are not heedless, to be deceived.

So very many unfortunates lost heavily, as it was discovered almost immediately after the death of Buncombe Hereford, that his whole estate had consisted in a quite fabulous series of hypothecations. At first it seemed incredible that it could be so, but when his colleagues investigated his affairs, they were astounded at the total failure to grasp anything of any value. There was absolutely not enough to meet floating debts on the unsettled existing current expenses incident to his household arrangements, or, indeed, of his funeral. But fortunately he left no one dependent on him except the poor crazy wife, or connected with him nearer than his cousin Alma, who, it was found, was his nearest of kin.

A few days after his burial, which, with the world, means literally the final disposition, or, one might even say, extinction of the deceased, Lennox was spending the evening at Mrs. Akmé's, where, as the *fiancé* of Alma, he was now a daily visitor.

They had been talking over the recent sad and mysterious event, when Mrs. Akmé said : " Lennox, I think the business affairs connected with the estate of Alma's mother should be very carefully looked into."

" I fear," said Alma, " it would be but a fruitless labor—without result."

" There are business methods of finding out," said Lennox, "and Mrs. Akmé's suggestion is very wise."

"For instance," said that lady, "let Alma give you a power of attorney to act for her, with which you can go to Virginia, and examine the records and see if at least some portion

of the handsome estate of her grandfather cannot be recovered. If taxes are unpaid draw
upon me for whatever is needful, or if the
amounts run into the thousands let me know."

"Oh, my best of friends," said Alma, "this
is like the love of a mother," and tears were
in her eyes as she kissed her.

"'Nor can I ever tell you as I wish to," said
Lennox, "how fully this tender care of dear
Alma is appreciated by me. Certainly I will
spare no effort to do as you suggest."

"When can you go?" asked she, "for you
must know, Lennox, that we women do not
like to wait. Call it impatience, if you will, but
what I wish done were better done to be done
quickly."

"I suppose," said Alma, "'go at once' ex-
presses it."

"That's just it," said Mrs. Akmé. "Men
don't know it, but we women supply the motive
power, men the mechanical action. They are
the automata, which, being well wound up, act
their parts as if they went of their own volition."

"That's rather hard on us," said Lennox, laughing, "yet we do play out our parts."

"Not often with any originality," she replied, "because tunes to order generally repeat themselves."

"But Lennox is himself," said Alma, content if she could save him from the imputation of not being clever.

"Of course he is," answered Mrs. Akmé. "I am discussing the sex in general, not our good Lennox. And after all is said, and very inappropriately too, for I have given him no time to tell us when he can go to Virginia."

"Unfortunately," answered Lennox, "upon thinking over my engagements, I cannot leave town for two or three days, but if, during that time, Mrs. Akmé, you will kindly come to my office with Alma, I will have a power of attorney properly filled out, as there is a notary public in a room adjoining mine, who knows the laws of Virginia and can do, as empowered to act, just what is needed for us."

"Very well," assented Mrs. Akmé, "it is

now Lent; we have but few visits to make, and to-morrow, Alma, we shall be quite at liberty, shall we not ?"

" We have no engagements for to-morrow," replied she, " and I shall be so glad to see the office of Lennox."

" Alma is so clever, Lennox," said Mrs. Akmé, " that she quite relieves me of every social care. What once often was a drudgery on account of the labor involved, has now become a pleasure. The dear child balances my visiting books, and is an admirable social accountant and in every way frees me from a weight of obligations."

" Yet it is so little to do," interrupted Alma.

" Besides," said Mrs. Akmé, unheeding the remark, " ever planning to help me, she has also constituted herself my little housekeeper, by trying to make me believe that I need more rest. So she interviews the cook, something I have always disliked to do, orders the dinners, inspects the kitchen and pantries to make sure there is no waste, **and gives us** a better table **at** less cost than I ever succeeded in do-ing."

"She is a rare treasure," **exclaimed** Lennox, his eyes sparkling with delight at this enumeration of Alma's good qualities.

"**There, now,**" expostulated Mrs. Akmé, "**why is it** that a man invariably grows enthusiastic when he hears of a woman who has the capacity to supervise the getting up of **a** good dinner economically?"

Both ladies laughed, and Lennox looked confused when **he** tried **to explain that he** " meant that **Alma** was a treasure *per se*, without a dinner—"

"Oh, **no!**" protested **Alma**; "only it's a pity that other girls are not allowed **to** manage their mother's households, and let **the** men see what capable wives they're losing."

"Why, Alma, you've grown diplomatic," said he.

" The best way, Lennox," **she answered, "is to give you a** bad dinner **to** test you."

"Oh, don't!" cried he, and instantly correcting himself said, "oh, do."

The next morning Mrs. Akmé and Alma, holding Chim in her arms, appeared at the designated hour at the office of Lennox Montague.

And now, in the marvelous chain of events, in which Chim had hitherto played a leading part in Alma's life, the hour was at hand when he was destined to reach the culminating act as her benefactor.

Who that notices the current of any one life straight onward as it flows, can ever fail to recognize a providential plan?

As a rule, every occurrence of importance that regulates one's destiny and forms a career comes, in its inception, from some unforeseen incident.

For instance, one most unexpectedly meets a person before unheard of, who exerts an irresistible influence on the circumstances surrounding one.

The homely phrase that "things turn up"

is expressive of this, and is literally true, for we don't exercise our volition to turn them; they rather turn themselves.

And yet, as reasoning beings, we know that there can never take place a result without a factor, a sequence without a cause.

But now, under the new conditions of the adventure of which Chim was to be the hero, he is about to assume, in addition to his former *rôle* of beneficence, the added title of discoverer.

And to be a discoverer is to perform one of the most illustrious functions permitted to mortals.

Columbus, Newton, Pasteur, Harvey, Rumford, Edison, are but the *alpha* of that star-set roll-call, whose *omega* stretches out into an endless future.

And Chim, through his acute sensibility, his fine nervous perceptions, and the exercise of that wonderful sixth sense, not given to humanity, may also claim the honor.

It happened in this wise, for no man is great,

or dog either, who waits not upon opportunity:

As Mrs. Akmé, Alma, and Chim entered the office of Lennox, he said, after the first greeting of welcome, " I know that it is, in a way, childish, but it seems so strange to see Chim here in Alma's arms; it oppresses me with a peculiar sentiment, if I may so use the word. It appears but yesterday that I happened to look out of that window, and saw the poor little skye for the first time, as the wretched performing dog of the organ-grinder. He looked then in that throng like an aristocrat out of place, yet perchance I would have passed him by without a second thought had I not recalled the remark of Mrs. Akmé about the destiny of the canine race. So I purchased him just in time for Alma to obtain through him the needed protection, and now, like a tie between the lonely past and the dear present, he comes back here with her."

While Lennox was talking, and thus giving a warm welcome to Chim, Alma was standing with the pet skye in her arms at the window,

absently looking at the throng of passers-
by that make F street so stirring.

As Lennox stopped speaking, she turned
and looked at him with that lovely expression
of mingled intelligence and candor that was so
peculiarly her own, while the exquisite blush
of the red-veined peach bloomed upon her
cheek.

" Ah, Lennox, memory this hour is indeed so
busy !" she said. "And what next, my faithful Chim ? What more can earth give than the
two who love me—my friend and my lover ? "

"One thing more," said Mrs. Akmé. "Chim
connects the past with the present, but what
can he do for the future ? "

And as they spoke, and Alma bent over the
dear creature caressingly, he turned his large,
responsive eyes full upon her, with an inquir-
ing look, that might have repeated, "What
next ? "

"We are all so preoccupied with our pet,"
said Mrs. Akmé, "that you have not noticed
this beauty of a desk—just see, Alma—it is a

gem in its way; come, examine it," and as she spoke, Alma crossed the room, and seated herself at the desk, but a moment later she drew back quite pale.

"Lennox," she said in a husky voice, "this desk recalls the days of my childhood." Then, scrutinizing it closely, she added in an agitated manner, "Oh, where did you get it? It is, yes, it must be none other; but let me see," and, stooping down, she moved out of their sockets the brass toes of the clawed feet.

"Oh!" she cried, "I would know it the world over; it was dear grandfather's desk. Oh, what a flood of recollections!"

And her face was all aglow with the delight of it. "Lennox," she continued, "when I was a wee dot, I loved to sit on the rug under this, and wriggle these toes. What happiness to find the dear old thing again! but the mystery is, how did it get here?"

"I bought it, Alma," Lennox answered, "in an auction room, and of course it was sent by some one for sale, out of the old homestead."

"What a record it would be," said Mrs. Akmé as they stood looking at it in an awe-struck mood, "if the history of the antique furniture brought to Washington could be written."

During the silence that succeeded this reflection, as Alma was seated at the desk with Chim curled up in her lap, he began to squirm about, point his fine nostrils, and fix his eyes intently on a certain spot. Presently a faint noise was heard, and Chim began to bark. "I have heard this movement once or twice to-day," observed Lennox, "but have been so preoccupied that I scarcely noticed it."

"It is a mouse," said Mrs. Akmé.

"That is bad," said Lennox. "There are valuable papers in these pigeonholes. I must buy a safe."

He had scarcely spoken, when Chim, who had been in a great state of excitement, with a sudden, almost feline movement, pulled away a small loose board within reach of his paw underneath as he sat in Alma's lap, where a mouse must have entered through some small chink,

it takes so minute an aperture to admit these
slender rodents ; it may have been no larger
than a worm-eaten knot in the old wood. Be
that as it may, as Chim dislodged the panel the
frightened mouse darted out, but not quick
enough for the terrier.

Ah, Chim ! a touch of nature makes all dogs
kin ! After all your graceful waltzing, your
Chesterfieldian bows, your drinking high-tea,
your fine table manners, your cultivated voice
for pronunciation and enunciation, your impro-
visations, your endless accomplishments, your
fine dressing, your calls made upon the élite:
after the endless training which caused you to
be lionized as the patrician puppy of the season, that luckless mouse disappeared down your
throat, and was crunched by those fine-pointed
teeth, so carefully brushed every day with London bristles dipped in oriental tooth paste—yes
even to the back bone crackled to a jelly—with
the zest of a gourmand over his *foie-gras*.

"Terrible !" muttered Alma, "so cruel too—
I wish I had not seen it."

" Yet Chim has done me a service," pleaded Lennox.

" Men are so cruel too, " moralized Mrs. Akmé; " they are never shocked by this killing—they kill game, entrap geese, ducks, birds, all living things, with murderous intent. It seems just despicable to me to shoot a bird."

"Oh, dear," said Alma stooping to look, "and you have broken the desk too, Chim—no end of mischief."

So Chim, knowing he had not pleased Alma, and thinking doubtless to regain her good graces, made a second pull from underneath as he heard a slight crackling noise, when there rattled to the floor some crisp leaves of yellowed paper.

Lennox picked them up, and, as he did so, exclaimed, " Alma, what next ?"

Chim, feeling that he had won his spurs and work was at an end, stretched himself out placidly on the rug, apparently unaware that his brow was now enwreathed with the laurel of the discoverer.

And as he tranquilly digested the mouse, three eager, flushed faces bent over those rumpled pages, with their ragged, nibbled edges—for just saved in time was her grandfather's lost will.

All these years that secret drawer had held its treasures—the hoarded papers kept by an overruling Providence for Alma—bonds, notes, deeds, securities, and her grandmother's exquisite miniature set in diamonds.

And the will was short, terse, clear, and legal. It gave to his only child, Alma's mother, everything, personalty and realty, in trust during her life, and in fee simple to Alma at her death, or, if Alma died without legal heirs, to his nephew, Buncombe Hereford.

It was then remembered by Alma that her mother had told her that her father had died suddenly of heart-failure, and thus this hiding-place was not known.

.   .   .   .

When Lennox, some days later, presented the will at the county seat in Virginia, there was no trouble in having it probated. Buncombe Hereford had paid taxes, and there were no incumbrances, although the large estate was sadly in need of repair.

One thing remained for Alma—to make the best provision possible for the insane widow of her cousin. But when the asylum was visited with this intent the suffering martyr had breathed her last, and the wounded spirit had gone forth to look down from realms of endless bliss upon this earth in pity.

And would the lost soul of her persecutor ever hear her accusing voice? Doubtless, at the *Dies iræ*.

.   .   .   .

Hereford Manor is now the home of a happy, happy family. It is a picture, in the mind's eye, of restful tranquillity. As the long, slanting sunset rays irradiate the fair scene, they quiver athwart the ivy-clad walls of the stately building, renewed by careful restoration to its prime. Under its friendly and hospitable roof again resounds the mirthful glee of children. And many family portraits look down from their places in the wide and spacious hall to welcome, as of old, each coming guest.

The well-filled library shelves are again reflected in the burnished brasses of the huge fireplace, over whose generous width is draped the quaint lambrequin, upon whose oriental texture rest the three weird bronzes, who still keep up their devil's tattoo. And there, surrounded by art treasures, sweetly smiles the picture of the gentle grandmother, looking toward the richly carved desk that stands opposite between the deep embrasures of two ample windows.

It has been renewed with loving touches, until the mellow tints of its dark mahogany reflect the forest scenes of Honduras in their depth of coloring, and the brass mountings rejoice in their mirrored surface when other busy fingers work with their wiggling toes, for ten little chubby digits at either side are hard at it, as the baby boy Lennox and his wee sister Alma are demurely seated on the floor, playing as their mother did with the pa-

tient old desk, that gives them the refuge of
more quiet work after a boisterous romp.

And Mrs. Akmé leans slightly on Lennox's
arm as they slowly walk up and down under the
superb avenue of forest trees, that are all aglow
with autumn's lingering, coruscating glory.

And she is saying: "Lennox, God is good.
He is great. I have faith in my heart, and
peace and joy in my life. And He has given
me therewith for the corporal works of mercy.
Nor am I childless, for I have a mother's love
for you and yours. Above all—thanks forever
be to His mercy!—the shadows of those
dreadful *isms* no longer darken my once
troubled but now joyful soul."

And as he kisses her hand, saying, "Dear
mother," they see Alma seated on the broad
veranda, looking out in her dreamy way over
the velvety, sloping lawn, over the well-
trimmed hedges, toward the deepening, richer
glory of the setting sun.

And contentedly swinging in a hammock
under some oak-trees near, is the dear old

gentleman from Little Washington, their loved and honored guest, to whom this happy family are forever, grateful for his timely aid to the poor orphan girl.

While their other benefactor, Chim, dozes on a cool straw mat at her feet.

He is growing old. He looks with the mild forbearance of gentle reproof upon the frolic-some antics of the children, although he lets them take no end of liberties with him. They flop back his dainty ears, pinch together his toes, pull his hair, which is getting gray, rub him up the wrong way, open wide his sleepy eyes, harness him with ribbons to a toy wheel-barrow, to drive a doll, dress him with shreds of all colors, steal his cream, then make him drink more than he wants, kiss him, pat him, hug him, tug at him, and he neither growls nor snaps, hides nor runs away, and never boasts that he was a gay dog when he was young that Washington winter. But he is discreet, as befits an old dog, although one can see at a glance that what he doesn't know is not worth the knowing. Nor does he ever hint to the children, "Pray who are you, anyway? I was before you were. Compared to me, you are as know-nothings." He spends much time in his old age with closed eyes that shut out the world's vanities, speculating as a Mahatma might, as to what is to become of him. And he ponders much, but still undecided, as to whether a new mode of annihilation will be invented for him, so that he may hope, according to his race, to reach nirvana? or is he destined finally to exemplify Huxley's theory of a soul divested of reason, that must die? This latter theory seems best adapted to his case, so by good right Chim is an Agnostic; and yet, had it not been for the elevating influences exerted upon him during the brief period of his life at the capital, he might, like many another dog, have lived and died without knowing himself.

The moral of this wonderful story of Chim's adventures being, that the highest attainable terrestrial plane may be reached within the possibilities of a Washington winter.